Curse of the Jack O' Lantern

R. BRIAN ROBBINS

Curse of the
Jack O' Lantern

TATE PUBLISHING
AND ENTERPRISES, LLC

Published by Tate Publishing & Enterprises, LLC
127 E. Trade Center Terrace | Mustang, Oklahoma 73064 USA
1.888.361.9473 | www.tatepublishing.com

Tate Publishing is committed to excellence in the publishing industry. The company reflects the philosophy established by the founders, based on Psalm 68:11,
"The Lord gave the word and great was the company of those who published it."

Book design copyright © 2013 by Tate Publishing, LLC. All rights reserved.
Cover design by Rtor Maghuyop
Interior design by Joana Quilantang

Published in the United States of America

ISBN: 978-1-62510-318-5
1. Juvenile Fiction / Horror & Ghost Stories
2. Fiction / Fantasy / Short Stories
13.03.13

DEDICATION

This book is dedicated to my children, Hannah and Ethan. You are my muses. Without you, this author would not exist. To my wife, Chelle. You are my strength and my partner in this process; your encouragement continues to propel me forward. You are the one who believed that this story was enjoyable to read and worthy of sharing. Thank you.

"Return of the Jack-O'-Lantern" took me the longest to write. I was stuck, and I could no longer see what to write. That is until the entire Robbins clan took an inspiring two-week vacation to San Diego in June 2011. One day everyone went to Coronado Island for the day, and I stayed behind working from a veranda from our rental that overlooked our secluded, private pool and the Pacific Ocean. I was in heaven! I was able to rearrange my storyline and finished off the leftover grilled salmon. A truly delightful day! I had found my way out of my lingering rut and finished the story soon after returning home. We had an amazingly fun time, relaxing with my family in sunny San Diego. Thank you,, Mom and Dad, for making it happen.

Finally, I would like to honor my late grandparents, Floyd and Virginia Raymer. Thank you for showing me (and my fourteen cousins) what true, unconditional love looks like. Grandma, without your example of loving like Jesus while staying young at heart, Grandma Bertie would not exist, and we would all be lesser for it. Thank you so much.

ACKNOWLEDGEMENTS

I would like to thank everyone who previewed my book in its early form and encouraged me to give them more. This collection of the *Jack-O'-Lantern* saga is the direct result of your desire for more. Thank you!

To Mark and especially Alora Westra, at Barnsignworks.com, thank you for helping me produce the images that I had for the cover art for all three books. Thanks for your skill, patience, and most of all your friendship.

To Paul Fedorchak, thank you for editing both "Return" and "Revenge". You helped smooth out some rough spots in both stories in a way that was seamless and almost imperceptible to me—almost. Thank you!

To all of you at Tate Publishing who have been partners with me in this process, thank you for your talents, professionalism, and the opportunity that you gave me to share my characters with the world.

A special thanks goes out to Miss Nydia Mathis, whom I have adopted into our family. In your mid-eighties, you are an inspiration, an author, a sculptor, a painter, and a teacher of language and living life to the finish line. One of these days, maybe my tongue will loosen enough to speak Spanish as freely as you believe it can.

CURSE OF THE JACK-O-LANTERN

1

It was another beautiful September day. The leaves were beginning to fall. The sun was shining, warming the cool air as Gus and Molly walked down Jackson Street.

"Feels like fall, doesn't it?" Gus asked his older sister.

"That's because it is!" Molly snipped matter-of-factly. "Yesterday was the first day of fall."

Gus rolled his eyes, arching his head away from his sister. "Oh boy," he murmured under his breath, thoroughly disgusted. "Sisters," he moaned, shaking his head.

Molly, equally disgusted with her brother's ignorance, thought, *I learned that when I was in first grade. He probably isn't paying attention in class, so typical of third grade boys.* She was a head taller than her brother, with long brown hair that sparkled with hints of amber in direct sunlight. Gus had dirty blond hair, which he often used as an excuse for not having to wash his hair during bath time. His reasoning or lack of reason always frustrated Molly as it had now. They didn't speak anymore until they finally reached the corner of Jackson and Lantern Streets.

Grandma Bertie's house was nestled there at the bottom of Jackson in a wedge between the two streets and the railroad tracks at the back of her property.

She had a lot the size of a football field compared to the concession-stand-sized lots of the other homes in the neighborhood. Their mother told them it was compensation for the railroad being so close to the house. The trains didn't bother Grandma Bertie much; she was hard of hearing anyway. Otherwise, she was in excellent shape for her age, or any age actually. She walked three miles most every day when the weather cooperated.

She had a large yard full of flowers, fruit trees, and her garden of fruits and vegetables of many kinds all kept in neat, clean rows. She weeded and hoed the rows every day. On Saturdays, she took a truckload of bagged produce to the Willow Branch Town Market for sale.

The kids would help her go to the Willow Branch Market whenever they could. They loved spending time with their grandma, but they also loved spending the money that they earned at their favorite stores in town. Molly always stopped at Brianna's Hallmark for the latest stuffed animal craze. Gus, on the other hand, would hit Jacque's Sporting Goods and then meet Molly and Grandma Bertie at Toys-N-Things before they all headed home.

Saturdays with Grandma Bertie were usually the only time they got to go to town during the summer months. And summer went much too fast this year. Gus and Molly knew the pumpkin crop meant the last of the market days until spring, and they didn't want to waste a moment at home when they could be at Grandma Bertie's.

Gus and Molly stepped onto the covered porch of Grandma Bertie's old farmhouse. *Creak*. The loose boards sounded eerie, sending chills up their backs every time they stepped onto that old porch. "Grandma, we're here!" They yelled in tandem so that she could hear them. But she did not answer.

They opened the screened door. *Creak*. "She sure needs some nails and WD-40," Gus said with an uncontrollable body wriggle.

"What's WD-40?" Molly asked.

"I don't know, but Mom says it makes loud things quieter."

"What brought that conversation about?" Molly asked curiously.

Gus stared at his feet for a moment before replying, "Mom said she wished she could use it on me sometimes."

"Oh," Molly said, nodding her head, "that makes sense."

Gus curled his nose and stuck his tongue out at her.

Molly looked at him with excited wide eyes. "You could get her that for Christmas!"

"Who? Grandma?" Gus chirped.

"No, Mom, silly!" Molly smiled. "Just kidding."

Gus looked at her with an expressionless face. "Oh boy," he groaned. They walked across the old wooden floor toward the back of the house. The new sliding door was open to the backyard. Molly saw her grandmother and yelled in complete distress, "Grandma!"

Her feet were touching the ground, but Grandma Bertie was slumped over a giant pumpkin. Her silver and white hair was in her face even though it was tied back into a ponytail. They ran to her. When they got close, she raised with a fright!

"*Aah!*" she screamed.

"*Aah!*" the children screamed back.

"You kids nearly scared me to death!" Grandma gasped, placing her hand over her heart as she leaned against the massive orange boulder-like pumpkin.

"We thought you *were* dead," Gus excitedly squealed.

"Didn't you hear us?" Molly asked.

Grandma Bertie felt her ears. "Oh nuts! I forgot to put my ears in this mornin' [referring to her hearing aids]. I was in such a hurry to get the truck loaded so that we could take this prize-winner to Thea's Restaurant when you got here. But I think we're gonna need some help," Bertie explained.

"We can do it, Grandma!" Gus said "All we need is…" His thought trailed off when he saw how high the back of the truck was. "Is Mr. Grogan's tractor."

Mr. Grogan was Bertie's neighbor who had a landscape business and a big white barn next to his house. He had farmed his two hundred acres for thirty-five years and decided to finally accept an offer on the land that would put what seemed like 1,500 homes in his backyard. He took the money and started his business, knowing that many customers were close-by and would keep him plenty busy in his "retirement." He had a lot of equipment in his barn, even a tractor with a front-loading scoop perfect for lifting 250-pound prizewinning pumpkins.

Grandma Bertie had the biggest prizewinning pumpkins and the tastiest desserts for thirteen years running at the Sycamore County Fair. No one could explain it; each year she would get one giant pumpkin in the garden, and Grandma wasn't about to reveal her secrets, as if she had any. If anyone asked, she'd say, "Must be livin' right."

Mr. Grogan made his way across the road with his scoop tractor. "Bertie, you know that if you ever need anything all you have to do is ask and I'll be there to help you." Mr. Grogan reminded her for the thousandth time as he loaded the massive pumpkin into to back of her truck with his tractor.

"Yes, yes. Well, I wasn't sure you were up, and I didn't realize it was so big," she chirped, referring to the pumpkin.

"Bertie, my lights have been on since five this morning," he said, looking over the top of his glasses, which had slipped down to the end of his nose.

He was a tall man with a broad barrel-like chest and large strong hands that resembled baseball gloves. His thick graying hair was usually covered by a baseball cap of his former school, the red and blue of the Kansas Jayhawks. The only time he took his hat off was when he was speaking with Bertie.

"I'll call. I'll be sure to call you first the next time," she said apologetically as she lifted herself into the front seat of her old red-and-white Ford truck. "I'll call you tonight when I get back. The Bensons want to play cards. Are you free?"

"I'll have to check my calendar," he said with a wink and a smirk, twirling his hat in his hands. He waved good-bye with his hat as they pulled out of the drive and headed to town.

A tired-looking crew pulled back into the drive that evening. The sun, still hot, was beginning to go down. "You kids want me to take you home now?" Grandma asked.

"Yeah, if you don't mind. I'm tired," Gus responded. Not a second later, he sat straight up and brightly asked, "Oh, Grandma, I almost forgot, can Molly and I pick out our pumpkins? *Please*," he said, nearly begging.

"Well, I think it is a little early to pick 'em. What are you goin' to do with 'em?" Grandma asked.

"We're going to make jack-o'-lanterns, of course!" Gus shot back. Bertie gasped so deeply that Gus and Molly, with their faces full of fear, thought for sure she was having a heart attack this time.

"You mustn't carve 'em yet. It's too soon!" she said gravely.

"Why not? What do you mean?" Molly asked nervously.

Grandma Bertie looked at them both. Her hand covered her mouth with a very concerned look in her eyes. Finally, she spoke as if she'd been hit in the stomach. Though she strained, her voice was just above a whisper. "Come inside. I've got somethin' I need to tell you, and it's too hot out here." Gus and Molly looked at each other with worried looks of confusion.

2

The oscillating fan that sat on a folding chair by the screened door twisted back and forth, creating a nice breeze into the kitchen, where the kids were seated at a round table. Grandma brought out glasses of lemonade for them as they waited patiently for her explanation. Dark clouds loomed in the distance through the sliding glass door.

"I've never told you this. In fact, I've never told anyone this story. A long time ago, there was a little boy about yer age who decided to carve a pumpkin into a jack-o'-lantern. It was late September, the week of the full moon. Well, as the story goes, he carved the pumpkin, placed a candle in it, and set it on the family's front porch.

"A thunderstorm came crashin', and at midnight, the full moon shone on that jack-o'-lantern. Lightnin' struck the front porch, and somethin' happened. Somethin' terrible happened that night."

With her big eyes focused on Grandma, Molly's stomach dropped inside her as if she was riding in the back of her mother's car on a bumpy road. Gus just stared expressionless at Grandma Bertie as she continued the tale.

"The boy's parents were awakened by screams comin' from their son's bedroom. They ran to his room. His door was open, and the storm was blowin' in through the winduh in his room. They ran into the room, and the father slipped on the wet, muddy floor. The sheets were pulled back to the foot of the bed.

"Mud covered the boy's bed, and a muddy path led out the winduh. 'He's gone!' they yelled so loudly and repeatedly that the neighbor across the road heard and came to see what was goin' on. They looked all night for the boy, and they never found a single footprint in that soggy, soft soil."

Both of Molly's hands covered her face, which looked a little whiter now. Gus filled up his glass for a second time as he waited for Grandma Bertie to continue. She cleared her throat before she spoke.

"They did find squiggly lines in the mud that ran from his bedroom to their backyard garden, where they found that jack-o'-lantern sittin' on top of a large dirt pile where none had been before.

"The storm stopped the next mornin', and the boy's mother looked out the screened door that faced their garden. To her horror, the mound of dirt that was there the night before was gone, but the jack-o'-lantern remained. It was the look in that hollow pumpkin's eye that frightened her most because it reminded her of her son.

"The boy was never seen again. And that's why I don't want you to carve that pumpkin until after the full moon in October. There's no reason to decorate for Halloween so soon." Grandma Bertie then leaned-in and whispered, "It's the curse of the jack-o'-lantern."

They sat and stared at each other for the longest time until Gus finally broke the silence.

"Okay, Grandma, creepy story, but I don't see what that has to do with me," Gus replied.

She smiled a knowing smile. "They call it the curse of the jack-o'-lantern because it is believed that the lightnin' strike or maybe the light of the full moon somehow brought that jack-o'-lantern to life. Some say it was the boy's fascination with Halloween that led him to carve a pumpkin so early, and they also believe that the jack-o'-lantern took revenge upon the poor soul that carved out its seeds, cooked them, and then ate them before the proper time.

"That poor soul was the boy who was never seen again, the boy who lived in this very house twenty years ago," Grandma added.

"You bought a cursed house?" Molly screamed, standing straight out of her seat.

"No, no, dear," Grandma assured her, patting her on the hand. "This house isn't cursed. It sat empty for years, of course. I needed a smaller, cheaper house after your grandpa passed away. This house was available at a very cheap price. And for a lot this size, well, I just couldn't pass it up. Besides, it was the only thing I could afford. I didn't hear about that awful story until after I bought it."

"Who told you?" Molly asked.

"Mr. Grogan, my—" Bertie stopped. Her mouth was wide open with a look of shock. "Oh dear, what time is it? I was supposed to call Steven to go play cards with the Bensons tonight."

Gus darted away from the table and returned in a flash. He huffed. "It's 6:25 p.m." Grandma Bertie had a clock in her spare bedroom. She did not like clocks; she had only one in her house, and it was located in a spare bedroom for the kids for when they stayed over on school nights. "Okay, kids, I gotta get ready and call Steven and—"

She was cut short by both children when they said, "It's okay, Grandma. We can walk home."

"We're rested now," Molly added.

Bertie looked at them both with a smile of gratitude. "Thanks, kids!"

3

They left by the front door onto the squeaky porch when Gus suddenly took off to the left, running around to the back of the house.

Where is he going? Molly thought. With her hands firmly planted on both hips. When she saw Gus returning from around the house a few minutes later, she knew. He was holding a pumpkin about the size of a basketball.

"What are you doing?" she shrieked.

"What does it look like I'm doin'!" Gus said sarcastically. "I'm taking my pumpkin home so I can carve it." Gus heaved the orange mass to shift its weight in his arms.

"Didn't you hear what Grandma said?" Molly barked as they walked.

"Oh settle down, will ya." Gus shifted the pumpkin again. "You worry too much. Besides, I'm not carving it tonight, so relax. It was just a story anyway."

"Just a story? Just a…I… I can't believe you," Molly stammered. "Do you think Grandma would lie to us?" she accused.

"No, of course not," Gus replied.

"What, you think she is trying to scare us?" she asked angrily. "No."

"What then? Is she hoarding all her pumpkins and their seeds for herself?"

At this, Gus chuckled and said, "No, I just don't believe the story is true."

Her eyes narrowed. "So Mr. Grogan is the liar then."

Gus simply shook his head and quickened his pace. The pumpkin was getting heavier with each accusation, and his arms were beginning to burn with fatigue. They walked five blocks in silence when Molly could no longer contain herself.

She yelled, "I'm telling Mom. You can't carve that pumpkin until after the full moon just like Grandma said."

Gus kept walking. *Only half a block to go*, he thought, not hearing nor caring what Molly had actually said. His biceps were burning more fiercely now.

Bursting through the front door, Molly ran to find her mother. Laying his prize next to the door, Gus collapsed on their front porch flat on his back.

They both now had something to prove. Molly believed that you should always listen to and believe your elders. Gus, on the other hand, believed everything must be tested. How else are you gonna know for sure?

Gus finally went into the house a few minutes later to find Molly still explaining the situation to their mother. When she had finished, her mother replied, "Yes, well, I think Grandma is simply trying to get you both in the holiday spirit, dear." She was smiling, rather satisfied with her response at such a complicated story. Molly's mother would never have said it for fear of hurting her daughter's feelings, but she actually sided with Gus on this matter. She didn't believe the tale was true either.

"Holiday? Halloween is not a holiday. It is a time of greed, ghosts, goblins, terror, fear, monsters. Shall I continue?" Molly asked without stopping. "Zombies, tricks played on innocent victims, vampires, deeds done in darkness, bats, spiders, cobwebs, parties held not in celebration but in hopes to keep evil spirits away. It is not something to be taken lightly, Mother! Besides, Grandma said it was true!"

Her mother and Gus stared at her blankly with a strange admiration for Molly's passion.

"All the same, dear. I think you are getting a little carried away," her mother said, still smiling.

"*Ugh!*" Gritting her teeth, Molly spun around, went to her room, and threw her door shut. *Slam!*

"Yikes." Gus looked at his mom to see what she would do.

"Never mind her, dear. Why don't you go outside and play before it rains. It is supposed to storm later tonight. We'll just let her cool off until dinner."

"Woo-hoo! Football, here I come!" Gus cheered as he sped outside with his football under his arm.

4

Dinner came and went without much discussion. Molly was still beside herself with disbelief of their complete disregard of her grandmother's story and warning. She was always silent whenever she felt mistreated or when no one took her seriously. She felt she had earned a little more respect than her brother, who acted out his every whimsy without thought of the consequences. Molly could not remember ever doing anything carelessly. Gus and Molly were both in bed and fast asleep by 9:00 p.m. It had been an exhausting day for them both.

Janice Johnson, Gus and Molly's mother, was cleaning in the kitchen when she saw the first flash of light. It lit up the distant skyline and was followed by a rolling grumble. The storm that had been predicted by forecasters for the last two days was finally coming through the area.

She toured the house for any open windows that needed to be shut, closing two on the west side of the house. Mrs. Johnson looked out the front porch windows; something caught her eye and made her nervous. *What is that?* she thought. The shape startled her. She could not make out what it could be, and she knew it did not belong on her porch.

Turning on the porch light, she peeked around the door as she cracked it open. With a sigh of relief, she chuckled, "Gus's pumpkin!" The sudden urge to surprise the kids with baked pumpkin seeds hit her like a bolt of lightning. Baked pumpkin seeds were a family favorite. She picked up the pumpkin and headed for the kitchen.

Crack! Suddenly, rain came down hard and fast as if it had been shot from a giant power sprayer in the sky. The lightning flashed brightly; Mrs. Johnson thought that all the streetlamps had magnified their glow for a few furious seconds. The thunder and lightning shocked her so badly that she nearly dropped the slippery pumpkin onto the tile floor in the kitchen. Her heart beat so forcefully and so fast that she swore it had actually stopped for a moment. She was out of breath as she thumped the heavy pumpkin onto the counter.

She was embarrassed at her response to the storm; she still felt insecure at night since her husband's tragic military training accident two years ago. Tears began to roll down her face as she lost herself in a memory and a moment of pity. And as quickly as it came, the moment was gone. She had stopped herself, wiping away the tears and taking a deep cleansing breath. *I can do this,* she thought. *I can raise these kids by myself. I am a marine's wife, after all.*

Turning her attention back to her task, she rustled through the drawer in search of her new carving knife. It was an expensive, sharp knife, perfect for slicing through tough, thick melon rinds, the young salesman had told her.

"Well, we'll see now, won't we," Mrs. Johnson said, grimacing as she glared at her prey. It was very late now, past midnight; she was tired but wanted to surprise the kids for breakfast. She placed the tip of the knife on the crown of the orange globe.

Crack! The house shook, and bright light flashed several times, blinding Mrs. Johnson through the kitchen window. Every muscle in her body stiffened into a spasm. When she regained her wits, she noticed that she had punctured the top of the pumpkin.

"You can do this," she giggled nervously to herself, continuing her mission. She sawed, ripped, dug, scraped, and lifted the slimy web of seeds out of the pumpkin and plopped them into a bowl. She quickly slashed a grotesque face upon the pumpkin with big triangular eyes and a jagged mouth. Mrs. Johnson stuck a candle inside the hollow pumpkin and placed it back on the porch, where she found it. The storm raged outside, and within an hour, she was headed upstairs for a shower as the seeds baked.

The water was just getting warm when she heard *crack!* Downstairs, the screened door in the kitchen was banging in the wind. She also heard something moving in the kitchen— or someone! She checked on the kids; Gus and Molly were still sound asleep. She found a ball bat in Gus's room and headed down to investigate.

5

Grandma Bertie and Mr. Grogan got back to Bertie's house as the storm began to unleash its fury. They had enjoyed a fun-filled evening playing cards and visiting at the neighbor's house.

"I'll see you in the morning, B. It's late, and I am beat," Mr. Grogan told Bertie.

"I'll say. We were beat all night by the Bensons," Bertie said, grinning to Mr. Grogan. "Breakfast?"

"I'll be over when I see your porch light on. Good night." Mr. Grogan nodded as he pulled his hat down tighter on his brow and raced across the road through the pouring rain to his front door and stepped inside.

Bertie watched with the porch light on until he disappeared behind the door. They loved each other. It was obvious to all who knew them, but neither one would admit to it. Being best friends was good enough for now. She made her way to the front room and plopped onto her favorite lounge chair to catch the nightly news before bed. Within a few minutes, she was snoring.

The wind had picked up intensity as the storm raged. The poplar tree at the edge of the garden was tall and wide but not deeply rooted. Strong straight-line winds lifted and pushed the poplar tree into Bertie's house with a crash. Bertie woke to the sounds of broken glass and rain splattering in her kitchen. She was shocked to see the top of a tree reaching through the kitchen's sliding door. Rain was pouring in, and she had to do something immediately to repair the problem. She knew she would need help. She reached for the phone to call in reinforcements.

6

A lightning bolt struck near Bertie's garden, and the strong wind that had uprooted the poplar tree in her garden had also opened the unfortunate tomb that held bones and a foreboding spirit locked in place for twenty years. That same unnatural and mystical wind blew through the garden, awakening the spirit that had been silent, dormant since the last time it was released.

That spirit-filled wind then blew through the neighborhood and forced rain onto the Johnsons' front porch and covered the newly made jack-o'-lantern, dowsing its candle inside. Lightning flashed, striking the front porch. Light flickered again from inside the hollow pumpkin, an unnatural, evil light. Its eyes flickered with rage, and its face contorted, altering its shape, revealing an even more menacing scowl. Green vines wriggled out unnaturally from its base, creating a torso. Violently, vines snaked out from the torso, spiraling into arms and legs, taking the shape of a human, and it began to move through the flower beds to feed its physical form on the soil. Nutrients filled its veins from the ground up, enlarging the creature's size and strength as it searched for a way into the house to find its seeds and the one who dared to again test the curse of the jack-o'-lantern.

7

A red-and-white Ford truck pulled into the drive that circled around to the back of the Johnsons' house. The cursed pumpkin slithered in that direction. It struggled, learning to move with each step. By the time the glowing form reached the edge of the driveway, the Ford truck backed out of the drive and sped away, not noticing the creature's presence. The jack-o'-lantern saw light through the windows, and it moved toward the front of the house again. It found an opening in the broken screened door that led into the kitchen. The flaming head seemed to be floating in the night as the rain and the late hour shielded it from neighboring eyes. It ducked into the house through the hole in the screened door and slithered into the kitchen, where mud from its vines mingled with mud already on the floor.

Flames shot out of the circular crown on its head and the holes upon its face when it saw the scene in the kitchen. Filled hot with hate, the jack-o'-lantern was enraged by what it saw on the counter and in the oven—its seeds! Recklessly, it knocked the bowl onto the floor, picking up as many of the seeds as it could and stuffing them into its flaming skull. The flaming pumpkin head knew more were missing, but by the smell, it knew that they would never be returned. The jack-o'-lantern's jagged mouth contorted, its eyes narrowed, and a great screeching noise came bellowing out its mouth, accompanying the flames this time. An extreme glow surrounded the monster as it searched the house frantically for the one responsible for this cursed deed.

The sound of running water came from up the stairs. With one hand wrapped around the railing and the other pressed against the opposite wall, the jack-o'-lantern pulled itself up the stairway, vine over vine until it reached the source of the noise. The yellow-orange flame inside its triangular eyes went black with hate. *Vengeance will be sweet but not swift*, the jack-o'-lantern thought as its vines turned the knob to the bathroom door and inched the door open; its vine-like legs were coiled, ready to attack.

Steam filled the room with a dense fog.

"The curtain, behind the curtain!" rasped a voice that came from another world. With one swipe from its bulging arm, the shower curtain flew open! No one was under the water; the shower was empty. *I must find the one responsible for this*, it thought. *And I will drag them back to the garden, and there they must stay and feed my revenge—forever!*

The garden was where the curse had begun so long ago. It began when a teenage girl was wrongfully accused of witchcraft and was sent to Salem, Massachusetts, a place where they knew how to deal with witches, according to the frightened townspeople of Willow Branch. The girl's mother was enraged by the injustice of the townspeople. She, being a true witch of the darkest order, put a curse on the lands of the whole town. All the land was farmland, and farmers for generations following the curse struggled to harvest healthy crops. Eventually, family farms were acquired by bankers and businessmen. The curse was soon forgotten. Today, only the corner in Grandma Bertie's backyard was used for growing anything other than the grass in the neighborhood that was regularly mowed by Mr. Grogan.

The morning was coming with the rising sun, and the jack-o'-lantern had to make a hasty retreat to that very corner of her garden before the sun withered its vines, forever breaking the curse upon the land. It quickly slithered down the stairs, out the screened door, and down the rain-soaked streets until it rested again in the soil of Bertie's garden.

Mr. Grogan did not see the glowing form slide into the yard behind the great root ball of the fallen poplar tree; he was too busy hammering the final nail into the last board covering Bertie's broken sliding glass door. Morning had come too quickly for them all this day.

8

The howling wind and the house-shaking thunder from the storm that raged through the night didn't wake Gus or Molly. They woke the next morning shortly after seven. Both were very hungry and headed down the stairs for breakfast. Their mother was always awake before they were with breakfast spread on the kitchen table ready for them. They felt she was magic for knowing when they would be up for breakfast. Gus and Molly smelled something burning coming from the kitchen. They hit the stairs running. The thick shag carpet covering the stairs was wet and muddy; the floor leading to the kitchen was also sloppy with mud.

They looked at each other with surprise. The kitchen floor was also covered in mud, just like the stairs! The place was a mess. Their mother was not there with breakfast waiting for them either. Everything seemed unnatural. She wasn't in the kitchen at all. The smell of burnt pumpkin seeds filled the room. They were still in the oven, and the oven was still turned 'on'. Molly leaned over the stove as far as she could reach to turn the oven off. They didn't dare open the oven; it already smelled bad enough. They were distracted by strange squiggly lines that spiraled through the mud covering the floor. The wavy lines led to the door with the screen torn out and hanging by one screw from its top hinge.

The squiggly lines reminded them of one thing—Grandma Bertie's story. Their hearts were pounding in their chests.

Molly's face grew tomato red as she turned to her little brother and screamed, "Did you carve that pumpkin?"

"No!" Gus shouted in defense. "I left it on the front porch!"

They both ran to the front porch. The front porch was clear, no pumpkin. Molly glared at Gus. He just shrugged his shoulders, and then they ran back to the kitchen. Looking at the messy scene, they both began to yell for their mother with conviction.

"Mother!" They darted from room to room. She was not in the house. They went outside and raced around the house.

"Mother!" She was not in the flower beds or the garden shed out back. She was nowhere to be found. They checked the garage. Their mom's van was still inside, but she was not in it either.

"Where could she be?" Molly mouthed, barely audible to her brother's ears. They made their way back to the kitchen and began to recreate what might have happened.

Looking at her brother, Molly said, "We can't get hysterical and jump to conclusions. What do we know for fact?"

"Well… My pumpkin's gone!" Gus yelped proudly.

"Okay. Wait!" Molly ran to the counter drawer and pulled out a small notepad and pencil. Numbering the lines down the left side of the page, she was again ready for the facts. She spoke as she wrote:

1. Pumpkin missing

2. Kitchen a mess

3. Pumpkin seeds in oven and on kitchen floor

4. Strange squiggly lines in mud leading outside the screened door

5. Mom's missing

When she finished, Molly hung her head and began to sob.

"What? What's wrong?" Gus asked, unsure why she was crying.

"Don't you see? It's the curse of the jack-o'-lantern!" Molly blubbered.

"Don't jump to conclusions, huh!" Gus looked at his sister; contempt was covering his face. Gus shot back sarcastically, "Come on, Mom didn't get taken by a creepy pumpkin person! Get real!"

"No, you get real. It happened just like Grandma said, and now she is gone!" Molly spit out the words and began to wail again.

"Let's call Grandma. Mom probably went for a long walk and is there right now," Gus said, trying to calm his sister. She was beginning to worry him; she was taking Grandma's story entirely too seriously.

9

The phone rang in Grandma Bertie's kitchen. "Could you get that, dear?" Bertie asked.

"Sure. Hello, good morning, Mol—what? How… Wait, wait. Hold on. I'll get your grandma." Steven Grogan handed Grandma Bertie the phone, shrugging his shoulders. "It's Molly. She sounds hysterical. I couldn't understand a word she was saying."

Bertie took the phone from him with a very concerned look on her face. "Molly, are you all right, dear? Your mother is missin'? No, no, dear, she's not missin'. A jack-o'-lantern didn't take her away, dear. She is upstairs in the shower right now." Bertie said, smiling with raised eyebrows to Mr. Grogan. "Yes, I know. She told me all about the mess. Seems the neighbor's hound got scared by the storm last night and crashed through the screened door, frightenin' your mother half to death, trackin' mud all over the place. She and the dog were wrestlin' around on the slippery floor. Your mother, bless her heart, finally drug that hound out the door by his collar. That's why the squigglies are on the floor," Grandma Bertie said, trying to reassure Molly. "What, dear? Why is your mother here? Oh, well... After she got that dog back across the street, she got to the phone just as I was hanging up. The storm busted out some of my winduhs, and it was rainin' in everywhere. I called your mom for some help. Her van's battery was dead again, so I came and picked her up. The storm got worse at that point, and we just got the winduhs boarded and the mess cleaned up a few minutes ago. And now she is washin' the mud off in the shower," Bertie explained.

Molly took a deep breath and a big sigh of relief.

Gus had his arms folded across his chest, gloating. Molly held the phone far enough away from her ear for both of them to hear Grandma Bertie shouting on the phone. She tended to talk too loudly on the phone because of her poor hearing. Gus had heard every word of the conversation.

"Told ya!" Gus beamed.

Molly turned, saw him, and gave him a scrunched-up mad face. "I'm going to take a shower," she huffed.

On her way up the stairs, she thought she heard water running. It seemed to be coming from her mother's bathroom.

10

Billowing clouds of steamy air engulfed her as she opened the bathroom door. Flagging her hands back and forth, she cleared the air as she made her way to the shower, which was running full blast on hot. The water was cold. Raging fury overcame her puzzled mind as the pounding of the water ceased.

"Why did you run Mom's shower?" Molly screamed down to her brother. "Now all the water is freezing!"

The steam had left the room moist with a film of water on every smooth surface. She stared frozen at a message that was scratched on the mirror. "Gus!"

"I didn't do it," Gus yelled, defending himself, as he walked in the bathroom. "What's wrong with you?"

She was staring at the mirror, looking quite pale. Gus's eyes bugged out as he read the muddy message on the mirror. They both stared at the message in disbelief.

SHE'S IN DANGER
BURY MY BONES
SAVE US BOTH

They dressed quickly and ran out of the house and down the street toward Grandma Bertie's. They did not know why but they figured she would have some answers to their questions. They did not say so to each other but Gus and Molly were scared out of their minds.

They ran around to the back of Grandma's house to the sound of a chainsaw moaning its way through what must have been a thick log. Mr. Grogan was cutting up the tree that had fallen into Grandma's house.

"Where's Grandma?" Molly panted.

"She took your mom to get a new battery and then was taking her home. She should be back at any moment now. What are you two up to this mornin'?" Mr. Grogan replied, wiping the sweat from his brow.

"Uh...um… We need to talk with Grandma about something, something important. We couldn't wait." Molly glared at Gus for responding out of turn.

"What happened to the tree?" Molly asked, trying to change the subject. "It was so big."

"Size doesn't matter much if your roots aren't deep enough. The storm pushed this big fella right over last night," said Mr. Grogan. "It's a shame. It was the largest thirteen-year-old tree I'd ever seen. Your grandma had me plant it just after she moved into this place. A real shame."

"Storm?" Gus and Molly exclaimed under their breath, looking intently at each other. Mr. Grogan didn't hear or notice them; he was still going on about the loss of the tree. In the driveway, gravel crunched under truck tires, signaling to the kids that Grandma was home.

She slid out of her seat with her phone to her ear.

"They're over here, dear. I'll bring 'em home shortly. Love ya too. Bye now." Grandma Bertie clapped her phone shut. "Hey, kids, yer mom was wonderin' where ya were." She noticed right away that they were acting a little peculiar. "Everythin' awright?"

"Yes. No. We don't know, but we don't think so, Grandma," Molly spoke up.

"You kids come inside. I'm gettin' ready to fix some breakfas' an' ya can tell me what's on yer mind. Awright?"

"Okay," they both droned nervously.

Waffles, bacon, eggs, and plenty of orange juice hit the spot for everyone after a long night for Grandma and Mr. Grogan and a frightful morning for the kids. Over breakfast, they relayed that they feared the curse was real before they had called her earlier and that now, after having seen the message smeared on the wet mirror, they knew it to be true.

Grandma Bertie looked at Gus and Molly as if she was peering through them both, searching for something hidden. She turned in her chair to look out her sliding glass door only to see plywood that covered the hole left by the fallen tree.

"Grandma, it is real, isn't it?" Molly asked about the curse with a shaky voice. "You do believe us, don't you?"

Grandma Bertie got up from the table without answering her.

"Follow me," she said matter-of-factly. They headed out the front door and around the side toward the backyard straight to the garden. "Kids, I have dug in this here garden for ten years since hearin' that story. An' though yer story does worry me, I have never found even a single bone chip in all that time." She stared at them both with almost a defeated look about her. "I don' know what to tell ya."

They stared at all the pumpkins in her patch, standing at the root ball of the fallen poplar tree. None of them could believe such an unbelievable story could have them staring at garden plants for answers. How ridiculous they all felt standing there in the wet grass.

11

The kids heard the grumble of distant thunder as they got into Grandma Bertie's truck and headed back toward home. Soon, rain began to plop sporadically on the garden dirt. The jack-o'-lantern spun its gourd head around to face the place where the voices had been. It had covered its carved crown with a couple of its leaves, camouflaging itself among the yet-dormant, lifeless pumpkins of Bertie's garden. The clouds overhead were thick and seemed to go on forever. The jack-o'-lantern began to pull itself up through the garden's silty soil. Moving under the protective cloud cover, it headed back to where it had been carved to life, back to the Johnson residence—for revenge. The sun would not stop its vengeance today.

"Now you two do me a favor," Bertie said, shifting the truck in to park in the kids' driveway. "Stay inside the house and keep the doors locked. Just in case."

"In case of what?"

"In case the story is true, Gus, and in case that message ya found was no hoax!"

"It's no hoax, Grandma," Molly replied somberly.

"Well, just be careful. Mr. Grogan and I are goin' antiquin', and we will be gone until evenin'. I'll have breakfast ready in the mornin' at seven. You comin' over?"

Grasping at something comforting in their conversation, they looked at each other, confirming and nodding their heads in response to their grandmother's invitation.

"Can Mom come too?" Gus quickly asked, sliding down out of the truck seat before racing to the house, trying to dodge every raindrop.

"Of course, dear."

Molly sat at the edge of the seat, ready to follow her brother inside when she turned and asked her grandmother a question that had been gnawing at her since they left the garden.

"Grandma, you never found any evidence that the boy's bones were ever in the garden, right?"

"Yes, dear. And believe me, I was lookin' every spring we worked the soil."

"Mr. Grogan said the tree that fell had been there since you had moved into the house?"

"Yes, dear. What is on yer mind, child?"

"Oh, I dunno, Grandma. Just thinking out loud, I guess. See you in the morning." Molly slammed the door and sped through the rain as it began to come down heavier.

12

Mrs. Timmons screamed! Lightning flashed again, and Mrs. Timmons, an eighty-year-old widow who lived two doors down from the Johnsons, screamed again at the glowing head staring back at her through her living room window.

"Darn kids!" She got up, wobbled across the room, and looked out her window. Straining to see through the heavy downpour, she saw nothing. She looked back at her glass of gin. The feeble woman wobbled slowly over to her special cabinet, put the bottle of gin back inside, and closed the door. She decided that a nap might help her gain her wits again.

"I need a different hobby," she said as she shuffled to her couch. "Maybe I'll take up racquetball? Something to keep my mind sharp and my blood moving, then I probably wouldn't see glowing pumpkin heads staring at me before lunchtime. That's what I'll do. I'll join the Willow Branch Health Spa…as soon as I wake up from my nap. Join the spa, that's gonna cost me. Darn kids," she mumbled as she fell asleep on her couch.

The jack-o'-lantern was making its way through the neighborhood to the Johnsons' house one yard, one flower bed at a time.

Gus was afraid of thunder and lightning as are most kids his age. Molly was too engrossed in her thoughts to notice the storm or Gus cowering under the couch blankets.

"Gus, I've been thinking." Molly looked at her brother. "I think the boy's bones are under that tree that fell by Grandma's garden."

"Yeah, so?"

"So we've got to go back there and find out for sure. Mom's life may be at stake, ours too if this isn't our imagination getting the best of us."

"I was afraid you'd say that," Gus whimpered as another lightning bolt lit up the room with a loud boom. "But Grandma told us to stay here." He pleaded.

Molly gave him the look; her head was tilted forward, and her eyes were piercing his will, full of fury.

"Okay, I'm comin'," he said in a defeated tone.

Their mother was curled up asleep on the sofa. Molly tiptoed to her, placing a small fleece blanket over her mother, and tiptoed back to Gus, who was now standing in the kitchen.

"Okay, Mom's asleep and should be out for a while since she didn't get any sleep last night. Let's go so we can get back before she wakes up and wonders where we are."

Gus looked at his sister before opening the broken screen door. "What do we do if we find the bones?"

"Right! I forgot. Thanks for reminding me!" Molly ran to the garage and picked up her dad's three-foot folding military shovel and stuffed it into her backpack with her flashlight.

"Let's go!" she said in a huff as she caught up with Gus.

"But what do we do with the bones if we find them?" Gus asked again.

Finally, she looked at Gus. "I don't know. We'll figure out something. We'll figure it out as we go," Molly said

They ran as fast as they could through the rain, which was blowing into their faces. They did not see the menacing eyes watching them from across the street. The flames within the pumpkin grew hotter with anticipation as the jack-o'-lantern crossed the street toward its prey.

13

A noise woke Janice Johnson, Gus and Molly's mother, from her nap. The clashing sounds of the distant storm didn't wake her; this sound was closer, more disturbing. This clashing was coming from inside the house in the direction of the kitchen. Momentarily paralyzed by the commotion, she forced herself up off the couch. Mrs. Johnson shuffled her tired feet across the carpeted floor toward the kitchen. At the doorway to the kitchen, she felt a chill come over her. The wind had thrown open the already battered screen door, and the damp, cool air was blowing in the rain. To close the storm door against the blustery wind, she pressed all her weight against it with a great struggle. Finally, it was closed. Leaning against the closed door, she dropped her head down, closed her eyes, and took a deep cleansing breath, trying to awaken more fully from her sleep-deprived stupor. She opened her eyes, and her heart was nearly stopped by the reflection staring back at her in the glass of the closed door. Mrs. Johnson felt another chill run up her spine like prickly needles. Her head filled with blood so suddenly that she felt as if her head would burst. The chill she felt was from the flaming pumpkin head across the kitchen floor staring at her face-to-face. It was a glowing jack-o'-lantern with green vine-like arms, and its legs were moving closer to her. The monster's gnarled vines were twisted into grotesque hands with mangled knuckles that were reaching out for her.

She turned to see it with her own eyes and screamed with all she could muster. Her dry throat did not allow her to be heard above a raspy whisper. Her plea for help went unheard. Before she could try again, she blacked out. She fell into its cold bulging green arms. Its sinister eyes, black with hate, glared at her for a bloodcurdling moment. Then from somewhere deep inside the cursed pumpkin came a small pleading voice.

"Momma, Momma, is that you?"

Another voice came from within the ghoulish gourd, a strong, deep, rasping voice.

"It's not your mother, boy!" it replied with a cruel tone. "She abandoned you long ago. Stop your whimpering! Soon she'll be joining you—very soon!"

Cruel echoing laughter filled the air as the monstrous jack-o'-lantern left the Johnsons' house, dragging Mrs. Johnson by the arm. It headed down the street back toward its nest in Grandma Bertie's garden.

14

Gus and Molly were at the hill on Jackson Street overlooking Grandma Bertie's house.

"We're almost there!" Molly cheered, looking at her brother. "And I think the rain is finally letting up."

"You really think so?" Gus questioned, squinting up at the crying sky, holding out his hand.

"No, I was just trying to make you feel better."

"Well, it's not working!" Gus shouted through the downpour.

They reached their destination, the roots of the fallen poplar tree. Molly ran to Grandma Bertie's barn and brought back a big bucket and a dusty burlap sack. She handed the bucket to Gus. "Here, you get the water out of the hole. I'll dig."

Several minutes went by, and finally the rain had begun to let up, allowing Gus to make progress, clearing the water for Molly to dig. The digging was easy. The soil had been softened by the rain, and it did not take long before they found the first bone. It was long and thick with a knob at one end. Molly picked it up; holding it in her hands, they both just stared at it blankly. It was the leg bone of a boy their age; he had been dead longer than they had been alive.

It was true. The story of the lost boy and the curse of the jack-o'-lantern were real. The reality drained them both of joy and of hope, filling them with emotions they had never felt before—dread of the future. They both felt remorse for something that they had not done and sadness for the loss of a close friend even though they had never known this boy. But what they felt most of all was fear. Yes, fear, fear of what had done this terrible deed to an innocent boy and may still do to them or someone else they loved, like their mother.

They finally looked at each other; neither one could tell if the other was crying nor if it was the rain running down their faces in streams. They chose not to ask.

"Keep working!" Molly yelled through the rain.

Soon they hit hard ground. Gus and Molly had picked up what they assumed was an entire skeleton of a young boy. They placed each bone very carefully into the feed sack that Molly had found in their grandmother's barn.

"Now what?" Gus asked.

"We have to bury them."

"They were buried!" Gus snapped back at his sister.

He's right, she thought. "I don't know. It's what the message said."

They were cold and soaked, standing at the corner of their grandmother's backyard. They felt very lost, unsure of what to do next. Out of the corner of their eyes, a comforting warm glow appeared. They turned. What they saw was anything but comforting; it was their worst nightmare. It was the cursed jack-o'-lantern dragging their mother behind it through the mud. Gus and Molly gasped, unable to move, frozen with fright, as their nightmare swished its way across the yard toward them at the foot of the fallen tree.

"What have you done?" it bellowed. Something inside itself had shifted. Something was different, and the jack-o'-lantern did not like it.

"What have you done?" Its eyes flashed even more furiously. The flaming pumpkin was puzzled. It looked at the muddy hole at Gus's and Molly's feet and at them and back at the hole then back toward them again. The jack-o'-lantern understood.

"No!" it howled. Taking their mother in both of its strong vine-like hands, it picked her up above its head and tossed her into the pumpkin patch. The pumpkins moved, allowing her room to land in the soft, silty soil. Mrs. Johnson began to sink through the muddy ground.

Overcoming her fear, Molly screamed, "Mother!"

"Give me the bones. It's not time yet!" the jack-o'-lantern screamed even louder, drowning out Molly's plea for her mother.

"No!" screamed another voice. It had both kids totally confused and looking around for its source.

"Bury my bones in sacred soil," the second voice was cut off by the first.

"Shut up, boy! You are mine until I no longer need you! You're mine!" The jack-o'-lantern howled, and a blast of flame shot from its jagged mouth.

"You can't stop me now! I am no longer in your cursed ground," said the mysterious voice. It seemed to be coming from the flaming pumpkin as well. The conflicting voices seemed to occupy the jack-o'-lantern's attention away from the kids.

"It's him! It's the boy who was lost in Grandma's story of the curse," Molly told Gus with a surprised look.

Gus looked at her with knowing eyes, but he still couldn't believe it was possible. A thunderclap followed another brilliant flash of light in the wet sky. Just across the railroad tracks, behind Grandma Bertie's garden, Molly saw the steeple of a church through a line of trees and houses in the distance.

Turning to Gus, she cheered, "I know what to do!"

15

Molly quickly explained her plan to Gus.

"Okay, but give me the bag. I'm faster."

Molly hesitated, reluctant to trust her brother with such an important and risky task.

"You're mine!" the jack-o'-lantern screamed in defiance and regained control of its limbs. Molly found her motivation staring at her with flaming eyes. She thrust the sack into Gus's chest. The jack-o'-lantern began to chase Gus, who was now holding the bag of bones.

Molly said a quick prayer for Gus's safety as she watched Gus lead the jack-o'-lantern away from the garden. She then turned her attention upon her portion of the plan—saving her mother.

She began wrestling with the pumpkin vines, trying to free her mother. Picking up her father's shovel, she ripped into the pumpkin vines, swinging it left and right, tossing green leaves and vine pieces everywhere. She was determined to stop her mother from becoming what the boy now was. Molly continued to struggle against the pumpkin vines; they were strong and determined to keep their prize, their source of life.

The pumpkin vines coiled themselves around her legs and pulled her to the ground. Molly was wrapped up and could hardly move. *You can do this. You are a marine's daughter!* Molly fought with a greater determination. She severed the vines one by one, some with her hands and many more with her father's shovel. Looking around at what she'd done, satisfied with her freedom, she reached down deep into the mud, grabbed her mother's hands, leaned back, and pulled with all her might.

Her mother began to move up through the soil to the surface; her face finally cleared the dirt, and Mrs. Johnson gasped for air. Molly hugged her mother, crying tears of joy, joy that Molly thought she would never feel again, and she cried even harder because she had regained their freedom. Their plan was working.

"What's happening?" Mrs. Johnson asked, still groggy.

"Mom, there's no time to explain. Come on!" Molly replied, pulling her mother to her feet. They ran together toward the rendezvous point where Molly hoped to meet Gus.

Gus was running for his life, weaving in and out of shrubs, jumping over hedges, and dodging mailboxes. He scaled many backyard fences throughout the adjoining neighborhood, narrowly escaping the jack-o'-lantern many times. Pumpkin leaves and pieces of vine trailed the jack-o'-lantern; it was not made to run. It should not be alive. But it was.

I better not get myself lost, Gus thought as he snaked a path through the neighborhood. *I had better head back toward the train tracks before this hothead catches me.* Peeking back over the last fence he had climbed, he taunted the creature some more.

"Over here, you overgrown holiday ornament!" The street was empty. "Where did he go?"

Green vine-like gnarled hands appeared at the top of the fence next to Gus's hands.

"Here I am, boy!" The glowing face popped up, screaming into Gus's face.

Gus screamed as he dropped to the ground, running faster than before. He was finally approaching the railroad tracks, and he was exhausted when he stopped to relocate the jack-o'-lantern.

Good, it's nearly a block away, but where am I? In his hasty retreat, Gus had gone down the wrong street and was much farther from his rendezvous point than he had hoped. He began a slow lumbering jog along the train tracks toward the distant steeple of the Willow Branch Catholic Church. His destination was now in sight, but he was out of breath, and the stitch in his side would not allow him to run anymore.

"Demonic jack-o-lanterns don't get tired, boy!" Gus twirled around toward the sound of the evil, guttural voice. His heart nearly stopped. The monstrous pumpkin's eyes were black as coal; it was on the tracks too and catching up fast. Gus's eyes grew wider knowing what else was coming. He struggled along as fast as he could, which, by this time, seemed a snail's pace to him.

16

The rain had made the ground soft, but it took all the combined efforts of Molly and her mother to dig a hole worthy of being called a grave.

"Where is he? He should have been here by now." Molly moaned, searching for any sign of her brother. "If anything has happened to him, I'll never—"

"There he is!" her mother shouted.

"Gus! It's behind you!" they both screamed.

No kidding! Gus thought, trying to will his legs to move faster. It was close behind him. They both were. The three-fifteen Highland Express was on schedule today, and it was coming faster than Gus was moving; so was the jack-o'-lantern.

Gus was within twenty yards of his sister, who was standing at the edge of the tracks at the Willow Branch Catholic Church. He knew he would not make it to them before he was overtaken. Gus did all that he could do. He spun the bag, and as he ran, he tossed it underhand toward his sister. He watched the bag fly through the air. It was a great toss, and it went the distance, landing at her feet.

The momentum of the toss threw Gus down to the tracks. He rolled over onto his back. A bright light beamed behind the jack-o'-lantern, flashing its silhouette in front of him. It was now five feet from him. The jack-o'-lantern looked up from Gus and saw Molly grab the bag and run to her mother as they entered the sacred ground of the church's graveyard.

"No matter," it mocked. "I still have you, little boy!" Its eyes flared in triumph. "All I need is your blood and your spirit will be mine! And with it, I will make a jack-o'-lantern army and fulfill the curse! All I need is you, and now you're mine!"

Gus's heart pounded as he leaped to his feet.

"No you don't!"

The train's horn blew loud, and its light shown behind the jack-o'-lantern like the sun. It turned. Flames shot from its head as it was completely surprised by the train's presence. The jack-o'-lantern had no time to react. Its jagged teeth were clenched in rage, and its sinister eyes were now glowing blue with an everlasting hate.

Gus jumped from the tracks into a ditch that ran between the track and a row of backyard fences. The train hit the jack-o'-lantern, splattering orange gooey pieces of pumpkin on the fences on both sides of the track. Some even flew over the fence into one of the yards. The train barreled over the green muscular body of the jack-o'-lantern, grinding it into nothing.

When the train finally clacked off into the distance, Gus checked himself, and he found just a few scratches. His legs, however, felt like they were made of stone, and he had a sore shoulder. He forced himself up with a great effort, and he lumbered down the tracks toward the churchyard.

"I guess Grandma Bertie knew what she was talking about after all," Gus breathed, rubbing his sore right shoulder. "Don't suppose Molly will ever let me hear the end of it." He chuckled. His thought changed quickly. "I never want to see another pumpkin again as long as I live." Gus's voice wavered boldly as exhaustion was overtaking him.

Molly and her mother placed the bag of bones carefully into the shallow grave and scratched enough mud over the top to complete their mission.

Bury my bones
Save us both

Molly and her mother stood hand in hand staring at the new gravesite as Gus joined them. They hugged one another with tears of joy. They were full of hope because they were together, and there was nothing they could not do together.

The next morning, they told Grandma Bertie everything that had happened while she had been gone. When they had finished with their story, she looked at Mr. Grogan and asked him to bulldoze her garden and to help her plant a weeping willow in Billy Gipson's memory.

"There will never be another curse of the jack-o'-lantern as long as I live, not from this garden."

Billy Gipson's gravesite was simple and small. The Catholic Church held a special Mass for him. The boy, who was lost more than twenty years ago, was now found and at peace in his new home. Heaven had been waiting.

EPILOGUE

Eight months later,

It was a warm, sunny day; Tammy was playing outside with her mother for the first time in two days. The rains had kept them inside, but today they were getting some fresh air and exercise.

They both had an urge to move. Tammy was five years old, and all five-year-olds need space to play and run. Her mother was expecting a baby in a few months; she also needed to stretch her legs. They were playing catch with a small rubber ball.

"Throw it to me! Throw it to me!" Tammy pleaded impatiently.

Her mother did, but the ball bounced over Tammy's head and rolled all the way to the fence at the back of the yard.

"Well, go get it," her mother encouraged.

"Come with me, Mommy," Tammy begged.

"Okay, I'm beating you!" said her mother, pretending to race Tammy to the ball.

"Mommy, what's this?"

Upon reaching the ball, they saw the strangest thing along the back wall of the fence. Large leaves with pointy tips were running along curly vines that were covering the ground. It was small, but it certainly looked like a pumpkin was growing in their backyard.

"Sweetie, this year I think we will have our very own pumpkin patch!" her mother said. "I wonder where it came from. We didn't have any last year?"

"Throw me the ball, Mommy! Throw it to me!"

Tammy's mother shrugged off the thought and attributed it to good fortune. She smiled at her daughter, bounced the ball to her, and wondered if Tammy would like fresh pumpkin pie. They played that day without a care in the world.

Pulverized pumpking stains were still faintly visible on the other side of that fence, the fading reminder of the jack-o'-lantern's existence. Birds, squirrels, and raccoons had devoured the remains of the cursed pumpkin that once lived.

RETURN OF THE JACK-O'-LANTERN

PREFACE

A seed is a miracle of nature that fascinates scientists, farmers, or anyone who has taken one, dropped it into a hole, and watched it grow. Transformation occurs in the dirt, and new life emerges from the soil to bask in the sun. All life comes from a simple yet complex little seed.

Given the right environmental conditions, even the smallest of seeds will transform into a plant much larger than itself with the ability to reproduce into many new plants. The environment is critical for a seed to grow into a mature tree or for a pup to become a fully grown bullmastiff or for a tadpole to evolve into a bullfrog. Environment also plays a critical role in the development of a newborn baby into a child and later a parent.

> A farmer went out to sow his seed, and as he was scattering his seed, some fell along the walking path; it was trampled on, and the birds of the air came and ate it up. Some fell on the rocks. When it came up, the plants withered because the roots had not gone deep enough to find moisture. Other seed fell among thorns, which grew up with the good seed and choked the plants. Still other seed fell on good soil. When it came up, it yielded a crop 100 times more than what was sown.
>
> Jesus of Nazareth, Luke 8:5–8 (NIV)

1

Ireland, 1845

In a quaint little Irish town, there lived Stingy Jack, a very foul man. He was known far and wide for the heat of his temper and the heat of the fires that burned in his blacksmith shop. Folks would come from afar to have Jack shoe a horse or repair a plowshare. His craftsmanship was unmatched.

Jack was never wanting for work or money, but his wife did. Jack's money flowed through Jack's fingers quicker than it flowed to their home. He never brought much of his earnings home. He lost nearly all of it gambling and drinking at the local pub.

Jack was a mean drunk and a very poor loser. He would leave the saloon only after wearing out his welcome and sponging off other patrons to buy "just one more chance" at the poker table. He was usually thrown out onto the dirt road in front of the pub. Jack would pick himself up with much effort and stumble along this road that wound its way out of town past the tree-line, finally coming to his little shack deep in the woods, where he took out his frustrations on his poor wife.

Stingy Jack accused his wife of hiding his money, beating her until she confessed or blacked out. For years, she lived in fear of Jack. On a cold and blustery evening in late October, Jack was on his way home with his largest—and only—winnings ever. A proud, boastful Jack sang at the top of his voice, so he did not hear the men who followed him from the pub and jumped him.

The men beat Jack, took the money he had cheated from them, and tossed him into the roadside ditch. Lying there near death, with his face bloody and his left eye so swollen that it could barely open, Jack could faintly see someone standing over him.

"Hel' me pweafe," Jack pleaded.

A man bent down closer to Jack's face and smiled. "I'm afraid not. It's time."

"Ti'e fo wha?" Jack slurred over his swollen tongue. His mind ached as he tried to understand what the man meant.

"You are finished, Jacky Boy. I've come for your soul," the man said.

"Who are you?" Jack demanded as his eyes widened and he sobered up. He rolled onto his back, staring at the man, whom he now knew was no man at all. Jack was staring into the face of death, Satan himself.

"Please," Jack begged, "I was going home to give my wife my earnings when those evil men beat me and stole my money. They are the ones you want. Please don't kill me." He cried at the feet of the devil.

"That's not going to work, Jacky Boy. You are no *saint*. Their time is coming, believe me. You'll be seeing your poker buddies soon enough."

Jack knelt with his hands clasped. He knew he had only a short time before the devil took him forever.

"Please, will you honor a few requests before I go?" The devil looked at his watch. He had a busy schedule that night.

"All right. Be quick! I'm not promising you anything." The devil scowled.

"Please look after my wife," Jack begged. "She deserves at least that much. And could I have just one more drink for the road?"

The devil was in a hurry. He again looked at his watch and began to steam in anger.

"Okay, but be quick about it," he growled.

Jack stuck his hands in his pockets and pulled out a small ball of lint and nothing more. "It seems I am a little short. Could you lend me a sixpence?"

The devil was furious. "You *are* a depraved soul, Jack, asking me for a loan."

Looking at his watch again, the devil reluctantly agreed. He transformed himself into a sixpence to speed up the process so he could continue his night of collections.

Jack seized the devilish coin and stuck it in his purse. He had tricked the devil. Inside his purse was a little silver cross. He had lifted it from the bishop years ago and kept it as a good-luck token.

The cross rendered the Devil powerless, unable to revert to his old self. Imprisoned in Jack's purse, he howled at Jack to release him. The always cunning Jack decided to make another deal with the devil.

"Let me live and I'll let you go," Jack said confidently. The devil reluctantly agreed and vanished into the night.

Jack held that silver cross in his palm and swore to change his evil ways. And he did. He stopped drinking and gambling. He treated his wife with the respect she so long deserved. He even took her to church every Sunday morning and back again Sunday evening. He made his weekly tithe and gave his earnings to his wife for safekeeping. Jack was a changed man—at least for a few months.

One night, while Jack's wife was away, he had the most frightening dream. The Mara, one of the devil's masters of terror, came to haunt him, manipulating his dream into a nightmare. He tossed and turned, trying to awaken, but the Mara, also known as the boo hag, sat on his chest, pushing the air from his lungs. Jack had thoughts of a life wasted in a church while his "friends" lived the good life at the pub. They were getting rich at the poker table while he slaved away over the fires of his shop. His wife was stealing *his* money, and he needed to get it back.

Jack awoke gasping for air, sweating beads larger than he had ever produced over his smithing fires. His mind tried to catch the thoughts of his dream before they vanished like the strange green mist of the Mara, who was hovering above his head.

Jack gained no joy from blacksmithing. As he toiled daily, he watched his friends leave the pub laughing at him and waving their cash-filled fists in the air.

He finally snapped.

Jack had succumbed to the tempter's snare. He stepped back into the pub for the first time in months, clutching a fistful of money.

Jack had forgotten about the life he cheated from the devil. He had forgotten about his oath to God and his wife. After a couple of drinks, he had forgotten most everything. Night after night, Jack stopped coming home to his wife, staying at the pub and losing his money. Frustration led to more beatings of his poor wife until finally, the lifestyle consumed him once again.

Jack opened his eyes and saw a man standing over him. The scene looked familiar: bloodshot eyes, pain, ditch, strange man smiling down.

"It's time, Jacky," the devil said.

Jack knew that distinct voice. He had been down this path. Not ready to give up his ghost, Jack asked for one small final request. Feeling more confident about his catch this time, the devil agreed.

"I am hungry and too weak to climb this apple tree. Would you get me an apple so that I may regain my strength for our journey?" The devil thought about his last encounter with Jack. He saw no way this would backfire, so he reached up and plucked an apple from the tree.

"Oh, this one is rotten," Jack complained. "Would you get one from up higher in the tree?" The devil snarled at Jack and stepped onto Jack's shoulders to reach higher.

"No, no, higher," Jack shouted. "I want the green one at the top of the highest branch." Jack motioned with his free hand.

The Devil climbed higher while Jack pulled out a knife and began to carve a cross in the tree trunk. The apple dropped into Jack's hand as the trapped devil howled. Jack once again made a deal with the devil.

"I will free you if you never come for me again," Jack said.

The devil reluctantly agreed again to Jack's demands and vanished.

Jack reveled in his triumph and became even more evil. He built a home in town, avoiding his shack and his wife. "Out of sight, out of mind," Jack told himself. His wife was a woman of nature, and he knew she would never follow him to town. He was free of her forever—or so he thought.

A strange man visited Jack's wife one dark evening. He was cloaked, standing in a shadow, and refused to enter the lighted doorway of her cottage. He informed her of a clan of women who would help her learn a trade and make her self-sufficient even though that was illegal in those dark days. The man reached out his gloved hand and gave her a book; he told her these women would help her to read the book that would empower her life. "No longer will you fear men," he said. He then vanished into the darkness as mysteriously as he had arrived.

Jack's wife found these women of the woods, and they took her in, educated her, trained her, and loved her into their sisterhood. They were educated. They lived off the land, eating greens from the wooded areas and glens. They made medicinal tinctures from the herbs they harvested and sold them to the townsfolk and weary travelers.

They met occasionally at night deep in the woods by a large bonfire, where they sang, danced, chanted, told stories, and even howled at the full moon. They were considered outcasts by most of the townspeople because of these strange practices. Eventually, they were persecuted for their behavior.

Meanwhile, Jack, who was cheating at cards, was caught with an ace of spades up his sleeve. He was shot dead in his chair. His spirit went to the gates of heaven but was turned away. Jack had lived a selfish life and had never chosen the path of redemption for his soul.

So Jack wandered the Irish countryside for some time. He grew weary and cold and sick to death of eating turnips, the only food allowed for wandering spirits. One day, he could no longer tolerate wandering aimlessly in the bitter wind; he finally decided to enter hell.

Jack was brought before Satan, who was sitting on his throne of ash. The devil recognized him and was on the brink of tossing him in the pit when a thought crossed his mind. *What if the others find out that this oaf tricked me twice? I might have a rebellion on my hands. For the sake of order and control, I'll have to banish him with a task so that I may save face and keep my reputation and my kingdom intact.*

"You owe me, and I want payback," the devil huffed. "You are hereby banished from my presence until you provide me with the soul of your wife as payment for the time you stole from me." The devil grinned. He wanted to test Jack's desperation, and he wasn't very fond of the lack of progress he was making with Lady Marguarette, the newest lady of the wood.

"I am afraid that will be impossible. I would never do that for you." Jack turned to leave but hated the thought of being cold for eternity, so he reached down and grabbed a piece of coal from hell's fire, stuffed it into the hollowed turnip he had been eating, and ran as fast as he could. The devil and his henchmen chased him but slid to a halt at the sight of Jack's little silver cross that blocked hell's gate. Jack had dropped it from his pocket purse so he could make his getaway.

The devil howled. "I'll get you for this Jack. When I find you, I'll tear you limb by limb. I'll find you if it is the last thing I do."

Jack ran and ran; he knew when the silver melted that all hell would break loose to find him. His hellfire coal would keep him warm, but now he had to hide from the devil and his minions forever. He needed help. Jack went to the only person on earth who might actually do that: Lady Marguarette, his abandoned wife.

Lady Marguarette still lived in her little shack in the woods and cautiously answered the pounding at her door in the middle of the night on All Hallows' Eve. Standing before her was her dead husband, Jack, panting, frightened, and asking her for help after years of torture, neglect, and abandonment.

She listened to his long pitiful story, debating in her mind what she should do. Revenge crossed her mind more than once, but her sisterhood taught her many ways to take control over her emotions and situations that seem hopeless, like hiding a dead man from Satan forever.

"I'll help you, Jack Smythe, but only if you promise to do exactly as I say without argument. Or so help me, I will take you to the devil myself." With his head held low, Jack agreed.

Lady Marguarette planned to head for the coast the next morning to buy a ticket to America. She sought to escape the horrors of the potato famine and the local townspeople who were capturing the women of the wood and trying them as witches. Hysteria had taken its toll on Ireland, and Lady Marguarette was ready for the freedoms of the New World.

What to do with Jack? She flipped through the large old dusty book that the mysterious man had left her, looking for an idea that might help her. And she found it. Jack was nervously looking out the window for unwanted visitors. He became more unnerved when she began to make a stew over the fire.

"What are ya doin', woman?" Jack yelped. She glared at him coldly, and he went back to watching the window. A few hours had passed; the sky darkened with the rumblings of a storm drawing near. Marguarette lifted the lid to the brew pot. She took one whiff and knew the stew was ready for Jack to drink, so she handed him a full cup.

"What's in it?" he asked, peering into the cup.

"If you must know, its willow root, bat tongue, potato skins, the turnip, and the ash that was inside."

Jack's eyes widened with disbelief. He curled his lip and flared his nose. "It smells like death!"

"It might save ya, ya wretch!"

"I'm not hungry," he protested.

She glared at him as he took the cup in his shaking hand. Jack looked out the window once more. Thunder had been rumbling in the distance, threatening a large storm. Jack peeked out the window as the first flash of lightning struck; he saw two large silhouettes running for the shack. They were too large to be human.

"Oh hell," he shrieked, downing the cup of stew. Jack backed away from the door, trembling with fear. The front door shook. The devil's henchmen were pounding on it in search of Jack. From outside, they heard screaming, coughing, and apparent gagging, so they ripped the door off its hinges.

Lady Marguarette was standing at the doorway, but they pushed her to the floor.

"Out of our way," they growled, looking around the one-room shack. "Where is he?"

Marguarette got up off the floor. She looked around, but Jack was nowhere to be found. She shrugged her shoulders toward her ears. The hellish creeps pushed by her again and headed toward the woods with a warning.

"We'll be watching you!" And they were gone.

Lady Marguarette saw them vanish into the woods. She searched the room, but Jack had vanished. On the hearth in a basket of gourds sat a turnip with a carved-out face.

"It worked. It worked," she sang to the frowning turnip. Lady Marguarette gathered her few possessions in a bundle, took the frowning turnip, and started walking for the coast. The storm did not dampen her spirits. She had successfully performed her first spell, and she was headed for the New World, where a new life awaited her.

Following a monthlong arduous journey by foot, sea, carriage, and horseback, Lady R. Marguarette Smythe walked into the small town of Willow Branch. It was dark, but the roads were marked with large orange gourds with a flame inside. She had never seen them before and was surprised how brightly they lit the path. The strange gourds gave her an idea.

She purchased a small piece of land with a quaint two-room cottage nestled in a nook of pine trees. She swept the stone floor and started crafting another stew. When she had finished, she took a cup and forced it down the turnip's mouth.

Marguarette changed one ingredient, turning the turnip into a pumpkin. She carved a foul face in it to remind her of Jack. She marched the carved pumpkin down a path from her cottage to the edge of the fencerow that wrapped around her home. She placed her Jack-O'-Lantern on the corner post.

Her neighbors asked her about the face on the pumpkin, which started a trend that spread throughout the countryside. They wondered what to call it.

"That's Jack-O'-Lantern," she said. "He's on the lookout for evil spirits. Best husband I ever had." Marguarette got a laugh from the women every time she said that and a cold stare from most of the men. She would simply smile in return.

2

It was 7:00 a.m. in the small town of Willow Branch. The sun was peeking over the tree line. A young girl with long, curly red hair stood on the sidewalk in front of an old white farmhouse. Her stepfather was not yet awake nor was anyone else at the corner of Jackson and Lantern Streets.

The girl's pale arms and legs looked ghostly against her black T-shirt and capri pants. Her oversized black work boots looked like clown feet at the bottom of her skinny frame. They clomped along beneath her as she marched toward the front door.

The porch creaked with every step. She cracked open the screen door, knocked on the solid oak door, stepped back, and waited for the lady of the house to appear.

The heavy door swung open, and a woman with short disheveled silvery-white hair pushed open the screen door. Her welcoming smile and misty green eyes met the marble green eyes of her student.

"Good mornin', Margie." Grandma Bertie grinned. "Ready to get started?" Margie nodded; her eyes were bright with anticipation as she stepped through the doorway without saying a word.

Melinda Dunn had been pregnant with Margie when she bought two hundred acres of woods from Grandma Bertie. Margie grew up with a natural love and appreciation of the outdoors. Her mother learned much from Grandma Bertie, so she taught her daughter about life and having fun.

Today was Margie's first class with Grandma Bertie. Margie wanted to experience what her mother had learned. She hoped she might understand and appreciate her mother even more by learning from Grandma Bertie.

"Today, I want to begin our herbology lesson with a Chinese poem. I… I think you'll like it," said Grandma Bertie, ready to burst with joy while staring at Margie.

Grandma Bertie led Margie through the kitchen and out the sliding glass door to the backyard. They walked across the spongy grass until Bertie stopped at the foot of a large weeping willow tree at the corner of what used to be her vegetable garden. She had a small book in hand. Its green cover was warped and faded, hinting at its age. Grandma Bertie began to read a poem, *The Leaf on the Water,* by Ouan Tsi (1007–1072).

> The wind tears a leaf from the willow tree;
> it falls lightly upon the water and the waves carry it away.
> Time has gradually effaced a memory from my heart,
> and I watch the willow leaf drifting away on the waves.
> Since I have forgotten her whom I loved,
> I dream the day through in sadness,
> lying at the water's edge.
> But the willow leaf floated back under the tree,
> and it seemed to me
> that the memory could never be effaced from my heart.

When Grandma Bertie finished, she glanced down at Margie. Streams of tears ran down her pupil's cheeks. Margie looked up at Grandma Bertie; their green eyes met. The next words were not even necessary.

"Thank you, Ms. Bertie. I loved it."

Grandma Bertie just nodded. Margie knew right then that Grandma Bertie was a special woman. Bertie knew what Margie needed and understood why Margie was there. She put her arms around Margie as they watched the weeping willow tree that reached for them in the gentle morning breeze.

"There is so much we can learn from nature if we take the time to watch and listen," said Bertie. "You must understand the delicate relationship between a plant and its caregiver. It is a sacred relationship—a sacred duty we have been given. If we love them and care for them enough, they will grow and reproduce many, many times. This allows us to use them in many different ways. For all the ills of this world, nature has an answer. The world and all that is in it were created for us, and we were created to care for them in return." Grandma Bertie took a deep breath and paused for a moment.

"I think what I'm tryin' to tell ya is that this is important to me and I hope our time together becomes as important to you as we go along." She took Margie by the hand, and they began to walk along the tree line.

"Margie, I've cared for this garden and others like it for many, many years, but this one—this soil—is special. Everything grows very well in it. I made it that way with hard work, dedication, and love. Sick plants become healthy again in no time in this soil. This willow tree is only two years old, and it is nearly as tall as my barn." She paused as Margie looked up at the tree.

"It usually takes a willow years to grow this tall. This garden is special, Margie, and so are you." Grandma Bertie cleared her throat and paused a moment to regain her composure.

"You are special because you are willin' to spend your time with me learnin' what I taught your mother. You are special because you are my...my..." Grandma Bertie struggled to finish the sentence. "You are my favorite student's daughter, Margie, and we're gonna have so much fun together!"

Grandma Bertie heard Margie's stomach grumble. Leading her by the hand, they headed for Bertie's kitchen.

"That's a good start I think. No sense gettin' too deep in the dirt on the first day. Now let's get you some breakfast."

Margie sat at a round table in the kitchen as Bertie pulled out bacon and eggs and warmed the skillet. This seemed like just the right moment to finally ask Bertie a pressing question.

"Ms. Bertie, would you tell me a story about you and my mother?"

Bertie was surprised by the timing, but she had been expecting the question. She cracked a couple of eggs in the skillet, threw in some bacon, and turned toward Margie.

"Well, do you know how we met?" Bertie asked.

Margie shook her head. She had already heard the story from her mother, but she was hoping for even more details.

"Well, my son brought her home from school to meet me. They were sophomores and needed someone to drive them to a school dance. James needed Melinda's prodding to get up the nerve to ask me. He had been grounded for rappelling from the town's water tower, so he thought your mother's presence would convince me to cave. He was right... Well, just a little. Your mother was a charmer. I could see why he fell for her. She was tall and beautiful with long, black curly hair."

Margie interrupted, "Did you let them go to the dance?"

Bertie smirked as she flipped the bacon and eggs. "No, not on a first date. Instead, I had her come to our house for a game night and dinner. We had a great time. Your mother was so smart. I think she won every game we played that night. Actually, I believe she won just about every time we got together after that.

She and I quickly grew very close. She would come over just to talk. And, sometimes we would walk through the woods where you live now so we could talk freely without James around."

Bertie placed two strips of bacon and an egg on a small plate and handed it to Margie. She sat down with her own plate and continued her story.

"They had dated for three years and were about to graduate when she came to me very upset. She said she had been doin' a lot of thinkin'. Although Melinda loved James with all her heart, she knew they could never be together because they were headed in different directions. She didn't know how to tell James without hurting him. I told her to let nature take its course. There's no sense prunin' before it's time.

"A few months later, Melinda left for college at Berkeley, and James joined the Marines. Their lives changed forever. James finally agreed to date others, but he swore to remain friends with Melinda. Eventually, James married Janice. Molly was born a short time later.

"Before the accident that claimed his life, James unexpectedly came home to see the family, but Janice and Molly were away for the day, visiting Janice's parents. James had lunch with me and decided to go to town in hopes of running into some old friends. He ran into Melinda at the gas station. She was home on break and was fillin' up her tank for the long drive back to California the next day. They spent the remains of the day reminiscing old times in the wooded confines at Lookout Rock until shortly after dark.

"When James got back home, Janice was so glad to see him. Nine months later, Janice gave birth to Gus, and Melinda gave birth to you a few days later. That's when she asked me to be your godmother.

"A short time later, my husband, Jon Johnson, died. I decided to downsize my life by selling your mother the two hundred acres that have become your sanctuary. I gave her a good price as a graduation gift."

Margie and Bertie were finishing their breakfast when Bertie looked out the door to see dark clouds rolling in from the west.

"I'll take you home in my truck, Margie. It looks like it's gonna be a gully washer," said Grandma Bertie.

Margie Dunn looked up from her plate and ran her fingers through her hair, pulling it out of her face to look out the window. She saw the clouds, but a little rain never bothered her. She smiled, remembering the long walks she used to take with her mother through the woods, the same woods where her mother and Bertie walked years earlier.

Margie and her mother would often walk for hours, talking and laughing. The worries of their world seemed to fade with every step. They would walk in the rain as long as it was not too heavy. During those moments, they ran. Sprinting through the forest, they would run until they slipped inside the Shelter Tree, her mother's sanctuary. It was an old twisted sycamore with a hollow large enough to comfortably fit a baby elephant. That was where Margie planned to go this morning.

"Thanks, Ms. Bertie, but I would prefer to walk home if you don't mind," Margie sweetly replied.

"Okay, but you probably should get goin'," said Bertie with great concern.

Margie was not the same fun, energetic, and engaging girl since her mother's death two years ago. Her spark for life was gone. Bertie knew Margie was headed for the woods and she knew why. Margie missed her mother. In the woods, she felt safe. It was a great place to feel the warmth of her mother's love.

Melinda Dunn, Margie's mother, had been heading to the Willow Branch courthouse to testify against Cutter Logging Company, which had been illegally cutting down trees on the land she had purchased from Grandma Bertie ten years earlier. Illegal logging was also under way on the forest reserve next to her property.

Melinda's car was struck from behind by a logging truck, instantly killing her. The Cutter attorney claimed the driver had lost control coming down the steep, curving hill. However, the brakes were tested, and no failure was found. Bertie sued Cutter on Margie's behalf, but the case has remained stalled.

A Cutter victory would mean the company could freely cut down all of the Willow Branch Forest, threatening Margie's trees and her favorite memories of her mother.

Margie finished breakfast, slid on her oversized work boots, and left Bertie's house. It was still early. Grandma Bertie started her Saturday classes at 7:00 a.m. so she could spend time with Margie and still catch a local 3K, 5K, or 10K run later in the day.

It was only 7:55 a.m., so Margie had an hour to kill before she would be ready to consider going home. Carl, her stepfather, went to work at the Willow Branch Mill at 9:00 a.m. She tried to stay out of his way.

Carl Hughes was a drunk and a mean one. Since Melinda's death, he only seemed capable of working, sleeping, and drinking and not necessarily in that order.

Grandma Bertie tried to get custody of Margie when her mother died, but Carl fought to keep her in hopes of a large settlement from Cutter. The judge was unwilling to grant custody to an elderly single woman even though Bertie was Margie's godmother.

On this Saturday morning, Margie left Grandma Bertie's backyard through the white picket fence behind the barn. She walked along the railroad tracks, headed toward the hilly woods to her favorite spot, the Shelter Tree, where she and her mother had spent so much time. It was the place where she would sit for hours, watching the clouds and reflecting on her mother.

Many memories were fading, so she valued her time with Grandma Bertie, who would rekindle the past. She dreamed of life today if her mother were still alive. And then she would cry.

As she kicked a stone, something caught Margie's attention in the corner of her right eye, beyond the eight-foot fence that ran along the railroad tracks. She saw the top of a small greenhouse with cracked roof panels. She grew curious and decided to check it out. A strange raspy voice inside her head said, *Yes! Come see. You might find something that needs you.*

"Yeah, I think I will," Margie said out loud to herself. Her spirits brightened as she looked for a way around the fence. She found a grassy path between two houses.

She entered a housing addition that ran along the railroad tracks. The house on her right seemed neat and clean—lived in. The house on the left was overrun with tall weeds and grass that had not been cut in months. She came to the street and turned left to walk to the front of the wild-looking house. Another piece of paper would not have fit inside the stuffed mailbox that had the name POWELL labeled on its outer wall. Margie bent down, looking at an envelope on the ground. It was addressed to Roger, Maxine, and Tammy Powell.

She looked around at the neighboring houses. They all seemed normal. *"This house looks abandoned. I wonder what happened to the family that lived here. Surely no one still lives here."*

She saw a narrow dirt path that slithered its way to a dilapidated greenhouse, sitting in front of a tall fence at the back of the yard. She cautiously crept toward the building of broken glass.

The open doors of shattered glass were hanging off their hinges like someone had left in a hurry. Margie peered inside. She saw a little red wagon with black rubber wheels in the back left corner. In front of her was a long, slender table that ran the length of the building. On it, she saw a pale green vine. Its tendrils looped and curled along the entire table. A tray of dry dirt held the plant. It looked strange to her. She had never seen a plant quite like it in all the woods or along any roadside.

Margie noticed it was actually two plants that had been spliced together at the stalk. The left half had big leaves like duck feet. Its vines were thick with long spiky needles. The right half looked more withered with vines that spiraled in all directions. On the end of one tendril was a small sphere that looked like a tiny pumpkin. *Adorable*, Margie thought.

"You don't look very well, little one. Did someone abandon you too?" Margie caught what came out of her mouth with her hand. She didn't blame her mother for dying, but she did still feel abandoned.

She reached to touch the tiny pumpkin, pricking her hand on a thorn. Or had the thorn pricked her, she wondered. Just then, an enormous burden overcame Margie. She felt the need to care for this little pumpkin, knowing no one else could or would.

"I won't leave you. I won't abandon you. I'll take care of you. Don't you worry, little fella. I know just what to do. I'll make you stronger than ever. I promise."

Margie pulled the little red wagon to the front of the table. She trimmed some branches and carefully slid the tray holding the pitiful pumpkin into the bed of the wagon. She had a new plan, a new purpose. She had one stop to make before she could head home and begin restoring her new little friend back to good health.

3

Gus woke up gasping for air as if he had been under water far too long. Panting for his breath, he looked around his room as if he was looking for someone or something. Just then, Molly, Gus's older sister, popped her head around his door. Gus squealed in fright at the sight of her.

"What was that?" Molly laughed. "You sounded like a chipmunk!"

"You shouldn't scare people like that," Gus shouted.

"*Sorry.* Mom says it's time you got up and had some breakfast."

"What time is it?" Gus asked.

"Nine."

"*Nine?* Wow, I still feel I could sleep for hours. I had the craziest dream."

"Another one? Was it like the others?"

"It was, but it seemed more real somehow."

"Well, you can entertain us as you eat your breakfast. Mom wants you downstairs *now*," Molly said as she headed to the kitchen.

"Okay, okay, I get the message." Gus flopped down onto his pillow, trying to recall his recurring nightmare. But the details vanished like a mist from his memory.

4

Margie pulled the red wagon loaded with her new friend to the side of her house, resting it below her bedroom window. She peeked around the corner to see if Carl's truck was still parked out front. The coast was clear—no Carl. She ran inside to her bedroom and raised her window. Margie placed in her closet all she needed to transplant her little friend. She reached out her window, took hold of the feeble plant, and hoisted it into her arms.

Margie heard a car pull into the driveway. *What's Carl doing home? I gotta go.* She quickly placed a clear plastic lid on her terrarium, clicked it shut, plugged in a full-spectrum lamp, and pointed it at her new friend. She closed the closet door to hide her pumpkin from Carl. She grabbed her backpack and hopped outside through her bedroom window. She was better off staying out until Carl left again or fell asleep. She felt safer that way. Margie had too many encounters with Carl when he was drunk. She couldn't take any more chances.

In his drunken, violent rampages, Margie reminded Carl of Melinda. He'd act like he'd seen a ghost. Then his fear would turn into rage. He would yell unintelligible words, throwing anything within reach at Margie or the closest wall. Lucky for

Margie, Carl was cut from the high school baseball team. His pitching was never accurate. She would run and hide in her room until Carl passed out.

He wasn't always like that, she remembered. *When Mom was here, he was a good man. But now, he is just hateful. Oh no! Who is he screaming at?*

Margie made her way around the house and crept under the open kitchen window, hiding behind the yews. Carl was on the phone, yelling as usual.

"You owe me! I've waited like you said, but the case is taking forever. This case may take years to finalize, she may never get any money and I'm sure your watchdogs are making sure of that."

Margie wasn't sure what she was hearing, but it sounded serious. She thought she heard him start to cry.

"I gave you the information you wanted! Why did you kill her? Why did you kill her? I did what you wanted. Now I want the money you promised me! And I want it now or I'm going to take what I know to the other side! I'm gonna get mine one way or another!"

Margie was in shock. She didn't know how long she held her breath, but her head was pounding. She gulped a deep breath. She was trying to fully grasp what she had just heard. *Carl had something to do with Mother's death? He must've given information to the logging company, which must be responsible for killing her. But why?*

Why had her mother been killed? She and Carl shared the same concern. But that did not stop her anger with Carl from turning to hatred. Margie shook uncontrollably as she again heard Carl's voice.

"Okay, I'll meet you one last time, but I'm having what I know mailed if something happens to me. You are not dealing with an idiot. I want my money in tens and twenties. Fine!"

Carl slammed the phone down, raced to his rusty old pickup, and sped away. Margie watched his truck disappear over the hill out of sight. She walked in a stupor up the front walk. She pushed the door open, took a deep breath, and began throwing anything she could lift.

She found Carl's prized possessions, his cases of beer in the fridge and his reserve stash under his bed. She took each bottle, one by one, pouring it onto his bed and favorite lounge chair that sat in front of his large-screen TV. Margie never played softball, but she swung a small sledgehammer like a champion. She made holes in everything she hit: the walls, TV screen, stove, mirrors, and windows.

She scoured all his drawers, dumping all his clothes into the bathtub. She poured lighter fluid over the mound of clothes and lit it on fire, starting the shower just before the ceiling caught on fire. She found a baseball bat in his closet, stood on a chair and bashed the smoke alarm to stop its hideous shrieking.

She broke Carl's favorite St. Pauli Girl German stein that doubled as his safe. She took $300, stuffed it in her pocket, and headed back to the kitchen. When every dish was in pieces, she went to her room, locked the door, and hopped back onto her comfy bed. Margie was exhausted, emotionally drained. She was determined to run away and never return. If Carl ever found her, he might kill her.

Margie knew she should feel afraid, but she was too tired to care. She threw her clothes into a large trash bag. Her suitcase was somewhere in the garage, but she didn't want to waste time searching for it. She reached down in her closet to grab her little friend but pricked her finger on its barbed vine.

"Ow!" She stuck her finger in her mouth, took two steps back, and collapsed onto her bed. She strained to open her heavy eyelids but couldn't. Her arms and legs felt too heavy to move. She strained again only to fall into a deep sleep.

5

Grandma Bertie's screen door creaked open. Steven Grogan, Bertie's neighbor and closest friend, peeked inside.

"What are you up to, Bertie?" he asked with a warm grin.

"No good as usual."

"Haha," he laughed. "Well then, I'd better come in and save you from yourself."

"Come on in. I saved you some bacon, and your eggs are comin' up."

"Bertie, what would I do without you?"

"Probably watch *CSI* all day and be bored out of your mind," she shot back.

"You know me better than that. I'm too busy for my own good these days. This neighborhood-lawn-care idea of mine is growing faster than I had anticipated. Nobody mows his own lawn anymore."

Bertie just nodded as she finished cooking his eggs.

"The bank called again. It has four more properties in fore-closure for me to tend," Steven explained. "This housing and banking scandal is really taking its toll on everyone."

"I don't know what you're complainin' about. It's keepin' you busy and out of trouble."

"You may have forgotten this, but I am supposed to be retired. I really need to find someone to help me with the demand. I just can't keep up by myself anymore. Problem is, nobody wants to work anymore. I may have to learn another language just to hire some help.

"Besides, just because you get creeped out by my favorite show doesn't mean you have to put it down," he scolded her. "I learn all kinds of useful things watching that show, and one of these days I'll prove it to you." He finished as she brought him his eggs.

"Well, maybe after you eat you can show me what you learned about trimmin' trees from that show. They're all growin' so fast, and I can't remember where I put my trimmers."

The trees had been planted where her garden used to grow. Bertie claimed to have the most fertile soil in all of Willow Branch—and maybe the world. But after the tragic incident that took the life of young Billy Gipson twenty-two years ago and the recurrence just two years ago, she vowed never again to grow a garden on this plot. The risk was simply too great.

Now she had plenty of time on her hands that used to be spent in her garden. She advertised in the local newspaper for students wanting to learn the intricacies of herbology—growing herbs for medicinal purposes and other everyday uses. She ran the ad for two months and got only one response: Margie Dunn. Not even her own grandkids were interested.

"It's not for everyone," Grandma Bertie told them when they had turned her down a third time. "It takes a very special touch to care for such delicate plants and unleash their potency and harness their secret powers." She tried to guilt them into attending class with Margie. Not even their friendship with Margie or their love for their grandmother could get them to think herbology was anything more than work.

Bertie began to cherish the thought of her time alone with Margie. She wanted the kids to know Margie even better but had become pleased about the opportunity to do that herself.

Between her time spent with Margie, Gus, and Molly, and her newfound passion of training for marathons, she was keeping quite busy and staying in shape—great shape for someone her age—or any age, for that matter.

Bertie sat daydreaming about her life as Steven ate breakfast. She envisioned the future. Coming to her senses, she questioned Steven about his thoughts.

"Hypothetically speaking, if you were to ask me to marry you and I said yes, what would you think about that?" Grandma

Bertie looked at him as if she were a three-year-old seeking candy before supper.

Steven sat back in his chair and stared at her. He was stunned and tried to determine if she was serious. He assumed she wasn't.

"Well, I believe that would be the end of our relationship, Bertie." He paused and then grinned. "I believe at that moment if I did not die of a heart attack, then the shock of it all would surely do me in." He smiled like a child that had been given candy before supper.

"Oh you! I'm serious!" Bertie snapped at him.

Realizing that he was wrong, Steven's expression grew more serious.

"Hypothetically?" he asked.

"Yes."

"I would be the happiest man in the world," he said matter-of-factly.

Bertie stared at him a moment. When she was satisfied that his answer was genuine, she went into the next line of questioning.

"Okay, how do you feel about having children?" The words crept out of her mouth even more cautiously than before.

Steven said and then coughed for a minute or two as a bite of bacon became lodged in his throat. "*Children?*" This one really caught him off guard. He thought for a moment that he was seeing stars. "Bertie, I'm sixty-six years old, and you…you… Well, you are in great shape, but you are older than I am. *Children?*" He was beside himself in disbelief.

"Okay," she continued without hesitation, "what about adoption?" He was still trying to figure out if she was serious or not. He assumed that she was this time.

"Bertie, by the time they would be in college, I'd be lucky to be alive!"

"Well, I'm not necessarily talkin' about a newborn, silly. What if they were much older?"

"Bertie, I, I… I haven't thought about this at all before now. I guess I am going to have to give this some serious thought and get back with you. I'm sorry." He breathed as if he had been hit in the stomach by a heavyweight boxer. She studied his expression carefully.

"All right then. I can wait," she finished. Steven took a deep breath and asked her a question of his own.

"Bertie, I think the time has come for you to be honest with Gus and Molly. They are old enough to understand. They love you no matter what. They deserve to know the truth. So when are you going to tell the kids?" His voice was loving yet stern.

"I'll have to get back with you on that," she said with a smirk. "Oh, would ya look at the time. I have to go for my run now. The Pittsburgh Marathon is coming much too soon for me. Are you coming with me?"

"No, I can't think and ride my bike at the same time. Besides, as I recall, I have some trees to trim." Their eyes smiled at one another. "I'll meet you back here for lunch," he said as he kissed her on the forehead. She turned toward her bedroom to get changed into her running gear.

Children, he thought. *What a woman.* His eyes were still twinkling as he watched her walk down the hall. When she had disappeared behind her door, Steven stretched his arms above his head. He got up from the table, placed the dirty dishes in the sink, and headed to the barn to grab the tree trimmers.

6

The sun was warming the morning air, shining brightly above the tree line as Steven made his way across Bertie's backyard toward her big red barn. His oversized hand dwarfed the old wooden latch that held the large doors shut. With a twist of his wrist, the barn doors swung open. The cool, musty air from inside the barn greeted him like an old friend.

"Now where would she have put those trimmers?" he muttered to himself as he looked around the perimeter of the barn. Rusted metal with wooden handles in all shapes and sizes decorated the walls in Bertie's barn—antique farming tools from the farm's past. They hung on the walls like gargoyles keeping watch over her beat-up old red-and-white Ford pickup and her new little scoop-utility tractor parked next to each other.

"Silly, stubborn old woman," he breathed.

Bertie recently purchased the tractor because she couldn't stand to ask Steven for help or to borrow his tractor. This frustrated Steven. He couldn't understand why she had the need to be so independent. He also noticed she didn't mind ordering him around. He didn't mind. He loved helping her because he loved her, and he knew she wanted the help; she just couldn't bring herself to ask.

Steven couldn't find the trimmers anywhere. He took a deep sighing breath as he looked up toward the rafters. There they were, cradled by two upward-facing hooks ten feet above the ground.

"Why on earth—better yet, how on earth did she put them way up there?" With his hands planted firmly on his hips, he simply shook his head.

"Now, how I am going to get them down is an even better question," he murmured as he looked for something to stand on.

Steven found a step stool, but stretching all of his six-foot-four-inch body to the max, he couldn't quite reach the trimmers. He found a large wooden crate against the back wall. He slid it over to the spot, climbed on top, and easily grabbed the trimmers this time.

He headed out to cut the tree limbs when the wall behind where the crate had sat cracked open on rusty hinges. He never knew the door existed. He peeked inside, but it was too dark to see anything other than cobwebs. Disinterested, Steven pushed the door shut and marched outside to complete his mission.

Placing the blade at the end of the long trimmer pole on the limb of his choice, Steven pushed and pulled until the limb fell to the ground. He reached to pick up the branch and place it on a burn pile when he noticed a hole where someone or something had dug. He stuck his foot in the hole, and it swallowed his whole boot. *One foot wide and one foot deep*, he thought. *Who would do this?* At the edge of the hole, he saw a partial footprint, and his eyes lit up. He was as giddy as a child at Christmas. He dropped the branch and ran like a teenager across the street toward his house.

Gus and Molly made a mad dash to the shed behind their house. Their mother had threatened them with helping her clean the house if they did not go outside to play. They opened the shed and pulled out their bikes for the first time in four months.

Winter had overstayed its welcome in Willow Branch, but today the sun was shining, and they were taking full advantage of it.

They rode around their neighborhood twice. Then they ventured across Garden Street into Deer Crossing, an older housing addition, to see if any of their classmates were outside. Of course, many were enjoying the sun on bikes, skateboards, and Rollerblades. Some were playing basketball.

Gus and Molly waved to their friends. Gus thought about showing off his basketball skills but instead decided to spend time with his sister. They passed Grandma Bertie a few times as she weaved through the neighborhood on her training run.

"Lunch is at noon if you want to come over," she yelled as they passed her. They couldn't get used to seeing her running. The shoes and tights were one thing, but her short new pixie haircut made her look even younger. She was always full of energy, more than they thought was humanly possible. She was teaching, training for marathons, taking classes online, and dating Mr. Grogan. She was busier now than ever.

They passed their neighbor, Mrs. Timmons, who appeared to be chasing Grandma Bertie. It was no secret in the neighborhood that she envied Grandma Bertie. She had lost every pie-baking contest and every sewing competition to her, and now she was trying to better Bertie in the Pittsburgh Marathon in a few weeks. Mrs. Timmons was determined to beat Bertie even if it killed her.

Gus and Molly rounded the corner of Jackson and Lantern Streets, racing down the steep hill to Grandma Bertie's house. Molly arrived first with Gus protesting that she had cheated by taking off before he was ready. She ignored him, hopping off her bike and walking it to the backyard.

Molly turned the corner of the house and saw Mr. Grogan stooped down at the base of one of the trees. They both laid down their bikes and jogged over to him to see what he was doing.

"Hi, Mr. Grogan." They both huffed.

"Oh hi, kids," he said, twisting his body toward them.

"What are you doing?" Molly started and then answered her own question. "You are making a foot mold, aren't you?" She beamed.

"Yep, just like on *CSI*."

"Awesome!"

"I think we have a thief." He frowned. "A few more minutes and this plaster should be dried."

"Why would someone want to steal dirt?" Gus asked, his face contorted in confusion.

"I think you both know that this is not just any dirt," Mr. Grogan said, looking over the top of his glasses that slid down his nose.

"Who would steal it? Who knows about the soil? And what do they plan on doing with it?" The questions flew from Molly's mouth. Gus and Mr. Grogan were paralyzed with which question to tackle first. A few moments passed in silence, and finally Mr. Grogan answered her while pulling the plaster mold from the ground.

"I don't know, Molly, but they wear Red Wing boots and appear to walk on their heels." This puzzled them all. They discussed the issue, and they all decided not to tell Grandma Bertie. She was very protective of this soil and had enough on her mind these days. None of them wanted to worry her needlessly, especially when they knew so little.

The remainder of the day passed uneventfully. Gus and Molly finally headed home after a long day in the sun. They were sure their mother would be calling Grandma Bertie if they did not get home soon.

The scourge of shadow crept across the valley of Willow Branch, bringing darkness as it passed. Gus was worn out from chasing his sister across the neighborhood and was snoring shortly after his head hit his pillow.

Molly was tired too, but the thought of the garden thief would not leave her. *Who could it be?* she thought. *Why would they have taken dirt? Did they know of its ability? What were they doing with it?* Her eyelids soon became too heavy to keep open, and her mind became too cloudy to think clearly anymore. The curse of night had claimed them all yet again.

The sound of voices in the driveway brought Margie out of her deep sleep. She could not see anything. Darkness was all around her. *What time is it?* Then she heard the voices even louder, and she instinctively held her breath.

"I don't care where. Just dump 'im so we can get outta here! On second thought, dump Carl behind those bushes by the house. No sense us trashin' up this fine neighborhood, aye, fellas?" Margie heard something crash against the house.

"Awright, le's get outta here before somebody sees us!" She heard two doors slam and a car drive off. Margie groped in the dark for her backpack. She found it at the foot of her bed. She slowly tiptoed to her window and slid out into the night.

Margie ran as hard as she dared in the shadows cast by the partial moon. She knew where she was headed. She knew the path by heart: across the railroad tracks, up the hill to the edge of the woods, left to the huge rock, and straight back, finally reaching the Shelter Tree.

The Shelter Tree was an enormous sycamore with a large cavity hollowed in its trunk. It was here where Margie and her mother would take refuge if a storm blew up during one of their long walks in Willow Branch Forest. Now Margie considered it her second home. She stayed there in the hollow security of their tree. She felt closer to her mother in the woods but especially inside that tree, which prompted longer visits. Carl's inability to cope with the death of Margie's mother without a bottle made Margie's visits more frequent.

Overnight stays were not uncommon for Margie; being unprepared was. She had packed all of her bedding essentials in a black trash bag but could not find it in the pitch-black of her room. All she had was her backpack for a pillow and her hoodie for a blanket. But sleep came quickly as she curled up inside the Shelter Tree.

7

Outside Gus's bedroom window, a strange greenish mist drifted through the branches of the maple tree. The tree's branches began twisting into tangled knots as the green formless cloud passed through them and slithered its way under the window that was left cracked open and through the screen into Gus's bedroom.

It floated across the room and hovered above Gus while he slept. The cloudy mist settled onto Gus's chest and took the form of a white-haired maiden with see-through skin. Gus's head began to twitch, and the maiden started to reveal her true form as she began to feed off Gus's fear.

Her white hair thinned into strings that hardly covered her head. Her skin became wrinkled and red with white flaky patches. She had the body of a small jockey, pointed nails like the claws of a cat at the ends of her slender hands, bloodshot eyes, and teeth that looked as if they had been filed into sharp daggers.

The world had many names for it: night hag, night witch, or the Mara, but the most common was nightmare. The Mara was chomping at the air above Gus. As he slept, she fed upon the fear she was causing him, turning his pleasant dream into a frightful and more disturbing nightmare.

She had been sent to scour Gus's mind. She was sent to find someone or something, and Gus had the answers she needed to give her master. Gus had to be encouraged to share what he knew—without his consent and without being aware of her intrusion.

Gus was running for a winning touchdown. He had nearly run the length of the football field when his side stung with pain. His legs felt weak. Gus didn't know if he could make it all the way into the end zone before he collapsed from exhaustion. A fog suddenly appeared before him, and Gus could no longer see the end zone.

He ran through the fog and smacked into a tall wooden fence. Using the cross boards as rungs on a ladder, Gus climbed to the top of the fence. Through the mist, he heard a familiar raspy, evil-sounding voice.

"Game's over, boy! You're mine now!" the voice screeched.

Before he knew what was happening, Gus was face-to-face with the flaming head of a jack-o'-lantern. *The jack-o'-lantern.* Gus could feel the heat of its breath. *Not again!* Gus's mind fought to wake. *Not you again!*

"Yes, it's me again, and this time they'll have to pick you up piece by piece when I am through with you," the jack-o'-lantern snarled.

The nightmare riding on Gus's chest became more animated as his fear increased. She fed off his fear as she rode. Her scheme was working, but she still needed more information. Her evil eyes turned blood red.

Gus tried to wake from his ghastly dream, but the Mara would not let him. His heart pounded harder; the hair stood on the back of his neck. He struggled with all his strength to break free from this nightmare.

Gus dropped to the ground from the fence and ran with great conviction through the streets of his neighborhood. He felt trapped in his own dream. Looking over his shoulder, he saw the creature chasing him. He swerved onto the railroad tracks. Gus had been here before; he knew he was close to the church where his sister would be waiting for him. He ran even faster, feeling freedom was close. But he tripped on the railroad ties and fell on his face.

He heard the voice close behind again. He slowly turned. The flaming skull of the jack-o'-lantern was six feet above him on a body of green muscular-looking vines. Its gnarled hand reached for him as a bright light appeared behind the jack-o'-lantern. The horn from a train distracted the monster as it turned away, allowing Gus to jump into the ditch next to the tracks.

The jack-o'-lantern exploded on contact with the train. Its pulp and seeds flew in all directions. Some fell along the tracks; some fell among the weeds and thorns. Some splattered Gus, getting into his mouth. One lone seed flew over the top of the fence on a soft spot of dirt.

Gus tried to wake up, but he couldn't. He tried to move, but he couldn't. He tried to breathe, but he couldn't. He felt like someone was sitting on his chest. He panicked. He was suffocating in his own dream. His heart raced even faster.

He got to his feet, climbed out of the ditch, and followed the fence to the front of an abandoned house. A dirt path weaved through tall grass to the backyard toward the fence.

Gus's legs suddenly gave out. There it was on the ground. He trembled in fear and disbelief. The jack-o'-lantern was staring up at him, surrounded by hundreds of pumpkins. Fire flew from its mouth as all the pumpkins began to climb out of the ground. Rising on vines that weaved into human shapes from the bases of their heads, they all stood before him.

"I'm back, boy, and I'm not alone! This time, vengeance shall be mine!" the ghoulish skull screamed.

Alarmed by her brother's screams, Molly burst into Gus's room and heard a strange screech. The window abruptly slammed shut, startling Molly. Gus flew up from his covers, gasping for air. He was as white as his sheets. He looked like he had seen a ghost.

"Gus, are you all right?" she squealed as she ran to him. Molly tightly hugged him as he struggled to discover his whereabouts. Slowly, his breath became more controlled. The blood returned to his face, turning it pink then back to its usual peach tone. His eyes began to focus; he now realized his sister was squeezing him.

"What are you doing?" he yelled. "Get off of me! Are you trying to kill me?" Molly let go of him, scooting away, shocked and a little embarrassed. Then she got mad.

"What were you screaming about?" Molly yelled. "You woke me up, and I came in, and you looked like you had seen a ghost." Her voice grew more concerned as she continued. "Did you have another nightmare? What happened?"

Gus's eyes were as big as saucers as he tried to remember the horrific night. But he couldn't remember anything. The Mara had accomplished her mission; the jack-o'-lantern was back, and the boy could be used to find him for her master.

Margie's teeth chattered as she awoke in the darkness. Her hands had a white, purple tone; they were so stiff from the cold that she could hardly move them. She suddenly felt a burning, stabbing pain in the back of her right leg. Her whole body twitched, and she screamed at the top of her lungs. She was sure a screwdriver was embedded in her leg.

Back and forth, round and round, she writhed in pain from the spasm in her leg. Leaves flew in all directions from beneath her. Margie rubbed the back of her leg until at last she could slowly straighten it. She heard the crackling sound of rotten wood beneath her.

I broke the roots! she thought. Then she fell through the rotten planks of the false floor at the base of the sycamore tree. Margie screamed as she fell, sliding down at a steep angle on an underground mudslide. She hit the bottom with a thud, knocking the air from her lungs.

Margie rolled onto her knees, straining for air. She raised her head to take a deep breath, and oxygen entered her lungs. She jumped to her feet, hitting her head on something hard. She fell forward on her face. She was out cold.

8

Dreams can be fun and marvelous. They have a way of appearing very real. Some people crave for them to last forever, but they abruptly disappear when eyes are opened.

Margie wanted this frightening experience to be nothing more than a bad dream—a nightmare. She feared, however, that the pain was very real.

She slowly opened her eyes; everything was dark around her. Her body felt bruised and sore all over. She thought it should be morning, so she did not understand why she could not see.

Margie's head was throbbing with pain. *Maybe that bump on the head made me blind!* She rubbed her head and collected her composure, deciding to test her theory before freaking out. She found her backpack beside her. She felt for the zipper, pulled the tab to open the main pocket, found her flashlight, and clicked it on. With that flash of light, she realized her nightmare was in reality her yesterday.

Margie saw a rope dangling in front of her face next to the large tree root she assumed gave her the bump on the head. The rope seemed to be connected somewhere above her, out of sight. When she pulled it, something shifted, opening a distant window above her. Light splashed down around her, exposing the cavernous room in which she was standing. The sun's rays shot back and forth in the room, reflecting off large pieces of metal staggered across the floor.

At one end of the cave, she saw what appeared to be a tunnel she hoped would lead to another way out. She saw tall baskets with lids lining one side of the room and smaller baskets in front of them. She walked across the dirt floor to the other side of the room, looking all around her. She was amazed such a place had existed right beneath her feet all this time.

Surely mother never knew this was here, or she would have told me. Looking upward as she marveled, she walked into something that knocked her to the floor. It was a large wooden table reminiscent of one Lancelot and Arthur might have sat around in Camelot. Margie thought it was strange there were no chairs in sight.

She returned to the base of the slide that had dropped her down into this underground chamber. Rubbing the knot on her head, she looked closely at the large root protruding from the wall that had given her the trophy headache. Something caught her attention: a large crevasse in the root with something inside. She reached in and pulled out a heavy bundle wrapped in burlap and tied with a thick leather belt.

Margie unhinged the leather strap and discovered two books inside. One was narrow, the size of a small spiral notebook. She held it in the palm of her hand. It was leather bound with a leather string weaving up the book's spine to hold the pages together.

She slowly opened the book, trying not to damage her new treasure. Surprisingly, the pages were not brittle. Instead, they were made from very thin skins and had writing too faint to read in the low light.

Margie tapped the flashlight against her palm. The light was a dull yellow, not the bright light she had anticipated. Margie slammed the flashlight against the palm of her hand, trying to awaken the batteries. *I knew I should have brought new batteries.* She placed the small book behind her on the table, focusing on the larger prize that remained in the wrap.

Margie eyed the larger book; it looked even more ancient. She could not grab it by the edges, so she slid her hands around it. Digging her hands farther beneath the book, she lifted it from its tomb. It was heavy—too heavy for her. With a great lunge, Margie heaved it onto the table, pinning her arms under its weight.

She struggled to pull her arms out from beneath the book. She swiped her hand over the top of the thick ornate cover to remove the dust. The cover had no writing, just strange symbols arranged in a circle inside another circle of raised leather.

Margie carefully opened the cover. The first page read,

**This book brings life to the living and the dead,
Nourishment for the mind and food for the soul.
The words contained within are powerful and mighty,
If understood and believed when read.
You shall receive power and glory, gifts from me,
As you shall be with me forever wed.**

This book belongs to:

Lady Marguarette
The Witch of Willow Branch

Margie repeatedly studied the first verse and could not believe her luck. She smiled for the first time in two years. She was so filled with excitement she thought she would burst. She had found a real treasure.

She flipped through the book, reading page after page of spells, incantations, and curses. Margin notes and rewritten phrases improved the spells. And then she found the page she was seeking: spells for reviving the dead. Her mind raced at the book's potential. No longer would she be bullied; no longer would she fear her stepfather. No longer would she be alone.

Margie had won the lottery; she had found her pot of gold. She planned to learn the book's secrets and use them for her purpose. Then a mind-clearing thought came to her. *I don't know who the Witch of Willow Branch was, but I do know who it's going to be!*

Margie's stomach grumbled. She placed the book in her backpack along with the small journal she had found. With great effort, she heaved the backpack upon her shoulders. She crawled up the earthen ramp that led to the sycamore tree. She had lost track of time in the cavern, but the warmth and brightness of the sun brought her back to reality.

The sun was high in the sky. Margie smiled again as she warmed herself in the hope that welled inside her. Then her stomach rumbled again, and her smile quickly faded. She knew she had to go home to get her favorite things—and her new pumpkin plant—before she could ask to stay with Grandma Bertie. She was starving and needed something to eat. She only hoped Carl would not be home.

9

Gus stared blankly at his bowl of cereal. He had tried all morning to remember even the smallest tidbit of his dream.

"Gus," his mom said, "is that all you are going to eat? Well, I guess it is. Look at the time. You've got to go or you're going to be late for school. Wait, have you brushed your teeth?" Gus ducked out through the garage before his mother could corral him. He sprinted to catch up with Molly.

Willow Branch Elementary served kindergartners through eighth graders. Even with all the new homes under construction, the school had room for more students. Built as a factory in the late 1800s, it had been converted and remodeled in the late 1940s after World War II. The Great Depression hit Willow Branch hard, closing the largest employer in the county. The building sat empty until grant money became available for a school. Brown brick and glass block windows towered over the campus. Inside, concrete block walls were matched with steel pipe railings to guide students between floors.

Teachers, students, and parents all knew one another—both the charm and the curse of a small community. The assistant principal called the parents of absent students and visited the homes of those who had missed more than a day because of illness.

Most parents appreciated Mr. Applewood's efforts. But students knew he delighted in catching them playing hooky then embarrassing them in front of the entire student body.

The weatherman called for a cool morning followed by unseasonable warmth and sunshine the rest of the week. Gus and Molly were climbing the steps to the front of the school. They passed Mr. Applewood, a tall man who was very well dressed by Willow Branch standards. He was not particularly attractive. His small piercing eyes, black thinning combed-over hair, and large aquiline nose made him look like an overgrown bald eagle.

"Is it me or does he look a little too giddy this morning, as if he is anticipating people skipping this week because of the weather?" Gus asked his sister.

"Could be right, or maybe he is looking forward to this last month of school as much as we are," Molly said with doubt in her voice.

"Maybe," Gus replied halfheartedly. "Nah, he's looking to bust somebody this week."

"He's going to bust you if you don't get to class on time. We are nearly late," Molly blurted.

Gus shook his head and rolled his eyes as Molly ran toward her class, and he strolled around the corner toward his homeroom. Gus sat down just as the bell rang. He looked around and saw every seat filled except for one. Margie was not in her seat this morning. Concern covered Gus's face. He wondered about the whereabouts of his friend on this pretty day. *I hope she's at the dentist. Wait, no I don't. I just hope she doesn't get into trouble with Mr. Applewood for missing school.*

The first three periods flew like the paper airplane that sent Tommy Miller to the corner of Ms. Barksdale's math class. Tommy was no stranger to school discipline. His mother taught history and also served as the lunchroom warden. Everyone knew Ms. Miller had a crush on Mr. Applewood. They had a common bond as strict disciplinarians.

Gus's head was in a fog, so he paid little attention to Tommy. Distraught from his nightmares, he had been foggy for months. Margie also seemed to be on his mind all the time.

Gus was headed to the lunchroom with his classmates. As they rounded the last corner, he saw his sister at the drinking fountain. Gus got out of line, making his way to his sister, who saw him coming.

"What's up?" she asked, puzzled to see him forfeit his place in the lunch line.

"Margie is not here today!"

"So?"

"So I just remembered we have a history test today after lunch!"

"What does Margie's absence have to do with your poor memory, Gus?"

"What?" Gus was confused by her response. "No! We have a test! She never misses tests! She's a freak like you when it comes to tests."

"Maybe she was sick today or had an appointment. I don't see what the big deal is, other than missing a test, of course. I wouldn't worry about her grades suffering. She is a good student, you know."

"I am not worried about her grades. I am worried about her." Gus realized by the look in Molly's eyes what he had said. "I mean, it's not like her to miss school. She hasn't missed since… since her mom died."

Molly put her hand on Gus's shoulder. "I've gotta go. Don't worry," said Molly. "We'll check on her after school if that will make you feel better." Molly grinned a devious grin, knowing she had steamed her brother. Gus stood clinching his fist as his face reddened.

Gus turned and sped to the cafeteria before the lunch line closed. The warden glared as he scooted past her to grab chocolate milk.

"You have ten minutes left, young man," she growled.

Gus sat in the only available seat—at a table filled with sixth graders of the worst sort. He dared not make eye contact for fear of being beaten. He was hungry and had to cram for a test. His sister was right about one thing: he had forgotten about his test.

At that point, Gus overheard Davon, a sixth grade bully.

"Hey, guys, remember that crazy girl? You know, the one whose mom died a couple of years ago. What a freak," he said, looking out the window with his mouth agape.

Gus looked up in fury. Then Trent, another creepy sixth grader, added to Gus's ire.

"Yeah, it must've been 'bring your daughter to work' week at the coal mine last week. Her clothes were filthy." The entire table of sixth graders roared in laughter because Margie's clothes had been covered in dirt from head to toe.

Gus was steaming at their cruelty. He opened the carton oof milk completely, raised his arm as if to throw a baseball, and showered them in chocolate milk. Gus tossed the empty carton at them also before he spun and dashed for the door. He passed the lunch warden in a blur.

"What the—"

"You little twerp. I'll kill you!"

"Not if I catch him first!" The entire table of sixth graders chased after Gus, but the warden stepped in front of them.

"Where are all of you going in such a hurry? You know there is no running in this lunchroom. What do you have all over you? Is that chocolate milk? I believe you all know the penalty for food fighting?" They all looked at one another and groaned.

"That's right. You can all have a seat until the last student has finished lunch." Ms. Miller scowled. "Then you can clean the entire lunchroom," she barked, turning toward the ladies behind the food counter.

"Ladies, you can go home when you get the food put away. We have some volunteers who will gladly clean the room for you today," Ms. Miller said with a sense of satisfaction. Just then, Mr. Applewood walked by, gave an approving nod, and smiled her way. Her eyes gleamed as she returned the gesture.

Gus didn't stop running until he slid into his seat before the bell sounded. He kept looking for Margie as the history exam was handed out. *Where is she?*

"You all have your tests. No talking, and good luck."

Gus would have to wait for his answer. The clock ticked too quickly. He was on question 15 of 100 with thirty minutes left in class. Gus was beside himself. *She's been home or playing in the woods all day!*

Gus grew more impatient by the moment. He raced through the test questions, barely reading them. He finished with eight minutes left, but two hours still remained in the school day.

Margie made it home, tears streaming down her face. *If the spell book is right, I can bring you back, Mom! Will you be proud of me or disappointed that Carl and I don't speak? Oh, I miss you so much. I wish you were here! If only you were here.*

She entered the front door, and her sorrow turned to anger. The mess she had made reminded her of Carl's role in her mother's death. She went to the kitchen, pulled out a carving knife, slammed the drawer, and headed for her room.

Margie locked the bedroom door behind her.

That's it! Take out all of your anger with the knife; use it and all of your hate will fade away—forever. Inside her head, Margie heard a strange raspy voice. The voice clouded her mind; it seemed foreign to her, but it also made strange sense. And it got louder. Margie looked down at the vein in her wrist bulging as she pressured the handle of her closet door.

Do it! Now! Before it's too late! Slash it! Slash it!

Margie opened her closet door. Inside, she could not believe her eyes. The tiny pumpkin had grown; it was bigger than a basketball. Her amazement was met with the voice in her head. *Slash it! Do it now!*

Margie exploded in rage, plunging the knife into her ghoulish white pumpkin. Again and again the knife came down upon the pumpkin. She cut a circle at the top and lifted it off. She stuck the knife inside, moving it in all directions. She then dropped the knife on the floor and reached both of her hands deep inside.

Greenish sticky, stringy muck from inside the pumpkin slapped the floor beside her. Her hands repeatedly dug and pulled out seeds until she had exhausted her energy, her anger, and the seeds. Margie gouged angular eyes and a hideously jagged mouth for its face. With one final movement, she placed the lid upon the pumpkin turned jack-o'-lantern.

Margie crawled onto her bed, trembling. She curled into a ball, trying to pull herself together. Her emotions no longer seemed under her control. What she saw on her bedroom floor made her shake uncontrollably.

An old rusted Chevy pickup pulled into the drive. Margie heard the engine backfire. *Carl's home!*

The gentlemen who had brought Carl home last had night profusely beat him within an inch of his life, but he survived. He awoke in the late afternoon, crawled to his truck, and sped off for the mill.

But upon his late arrival at work, Carl had been informed that he had been fired. His supervisor warned him to never again threaten the logging company's owners or it might be the last thing he ever did.

Carl struggled his way up the drive to the house. His left leg and his head were throbbing; he wanted a beer to wash away his pain. The front door was standing wide open. A wild-eyed and wary Carl hobbled back to his truck and pulled out his shotgun. He stepped cautiously to the door and inside, listening intently.

10

The final bell rang at 2:57 p.m. at Willow Branch Elementary. The halls exploded in excitement over the freedom they all felt at hearing the day's final bell. Gus briskly walked to his locker. He didn't want to serve detention for running—not now. He searched for his sister so they could head to Grandma Bertie's in hopes of finding Margie. Gus was on a mission. He needed to tell

Margie what nearly happened to him when he had defended her honor. He was focused.

Gus slammed his locker shut. He had nothing in his backpack except the jacket he had worn that morning. He weaved his way past students, zigzagging through the halls until he finally saw Molly at her locker stuffing her backpack with books.

"Come on. Let's go!"

With lips pursed, she glared at him from the corner of her eye. Molly did not like to be bossed around, especially by her brother. She did not answer.

Gus grew more impatient as Molly attempted to cram another book into her backpack.

"What are you doing?" Gus exploded. "You've got enough books. Let's go already!"

"I can't fit my social studies book in my backpack because I have tests in all my other classes," said Molly. "But I have to read chapter 20 for Thursday's quiz."

"So leave it and read it tomorrow night," Gus shouted. Molly frowned. Gus burst in frustration.

"Just give it to me! I'll carry it," he said. "I've got plenty of room in my backpack."

Molly rolled her eyes and sighed as she handed the book to Gus; he always had room in his backpack. Gus tossed it into his pack and hurried toward the front door.

Mr. Applewood was standing at the cafeteria door, talking to someone as Gus passed.

"Now, I hope you all learned your lesson today and we will not have to revisit this again," he stressed to the group of sixth graders. They smiled and nodded. "Okay, you may go."

They all saw Gus out of the corners of their eyes and yelled in unison: "*Get 'im!*" The boys had retaliation on their minds since lunch, and revenge engorged their collective hearts.

Molly, who was lagging behind Gus, heard the sixth graders. She spun to see who they were yelling at. The enraged boys were focused on Gus, as they weaved between schoolmates along the hall. They did not notice Molly turning in front of them. Molly's backpack swung through the air like the strongman's mallet at the county fair; once in motion, there was no stopping it.

Her backpack crashed into the legs of the running boys, spilling them on top of one another. "Run, Gus," Molly shouted. "Run!"

Gus heard Molly squeal and turned toward her. He saw the fallen sixth grade bullies. His eyes bugged out. He ran as fast as he could, weaving again through students waiting along the sidewalk for their buses.

Gus crossed the street and headed for the park that led into the neighborhood adjacent to Grandma Bertie's. Thanks to his sister's heavy bag, Gus made it to Grandma Bertie's in one piece.

Gus, huffing and trying to catch his breath, asked Bertie if she had seen Margie.

Just then, Molly stepped from the bathroom.

"How did you get here so fast?" Gus asked.

"I wasn't weaving through the entire neighborhood. I walked a straight path here. Gus, why were those boys chasing after you?" Molly asked.

"I have something to tell you both," Grandma Bertie sadly said. "You two will be stayin' here with me this week because your mother had a surprise interview in Minnesota, and she has to leave today." Gus and Molly looked at each other in bewilderment, and then they cheered with broad smiles. Grandma Bertie just shook her head.

"Come on, Molly!" Gus beamed. "Let's go tell Margie. Maybe she will stay with us, if it is all right with you, Grandma."

"That's fine with me. The more, the merrier." Grandma Bertie smiled. Gus and Molly sprinted through the screened door and headed to Margie's house. Gus had plenty to tell her.

Carl listened with all of his being but heard nothing. He crept through the front door and couldn't believe what he saw. The living room and kitchen looked like they had been hit by a tornado. Carl's eyes bugged and his jaw dropped. *Damn them! They trashed my entire life in less than a day.* Stepping silently as possible, Carl headed down the hall with his gun in hand.

His bedroom door was shut. Carl never closed his bedroom door or the shower curtain; he suffered from a severe case of claustrophobia—a byproduct of being locked in a closet all day by a babysitter when he was five. *Maybe they're still here, waiting to waylay me again.* His heart pounded even harder. With his hand shaking, he slowly turned the knob and flung open the door. Carl's bedroom was turned upside down. He smelled burned rubber wafting from the bathroom. He stepped over several empty drawers to reach the archway to the bathroom. A towering mound of blackened muck in the tub greeted Carl. He slowly turned and, looking back at the empty drawers, realized everything that should be in them was now smoldering in his bathtub.

"Oh no," Carl moaned. "This has to be my worst day ever."

Then his heart leaped inside his chest at the rustling coming from Margie's room. "Margie? Are you here?" He ran to her door and knocked. "Margie?" Margie stood up on her bed, grabbed the carving knife, and screamed.

"Get away from me! Leave me alone!" Margie was frantic. Carl wasn't sure why she was being so hostile toward him, but he was determined to find out. He tried to turn the knob, but it was locked. "Margie, you open this door right now!"

"No! Go away! Get out of here!"

Carl grew even more enraged. He stepped back and rammed the door with his shoulder. The door flew open.

"No, Carl! Get out of here!" Margie screamed, still wielding the knife.

"This is my house, little girl, and you do not threaten me in my home! Put that knife down, now! That's it! I'm gonna teach you some manners!" Margie was in the corner of her bedroom with her back against the wall. Her entire body was shaking uncontrollably.

"Go away, Carl, please," she screamed. She had a sick look about her, but he was determined she would show him proper respect. Carl loosened his belt.

He raised his belt above his head and swung it at her as he lunged toward the bed, knocking the knife from her hands.

"What are you doing? Get out of here!" Margie screamed as the source of her fear emerged from behind the closet door behind Carl. The flame-filled eyes of the ghoulish jack-o'-lantern were focused on its prey.

"I'm gonna teach you some manners, little girl," Carl hissed as he hit Margie with his belt. The jack-o'-lantern looked down at his newly formed body, admiring his gnarly hands and noticing something he had not anticipated. Thorns had grown along his arms and legs. He was pleased with this new feature, but he was very weak and pale. His skull was whitish green; he needed energy, sustenance. He needed—blood. The jack-o'-lantern seized the opportunity, wrapping its vines around his victim's throat.

Carl's eyes bulged in surprise. Another vine wrapped around Carl's wrist, preventing him from hitting Margie again. The jack-o'-lantern spun Carl around so he was face-to-face with his attacker. Carl tried to scream, but the jack-o'-lantern squeezed even tighter. A needlelike thorn emerged from the tip of the jack-o'-lantern's finger and sunk into Carl's neck. Margie fainted, falling back onto her bed.

Carl became pale as the jack-o'-lantern siphoned his blood from his body. The vines of the jack-o'-lantern grew a dark, vibrant green. Its skull remained a ghoulish luminescent yellow green. Carl's body began to shrivel as the jack-o'-lantern grew even stronger.

"Couldn't let you damage my prize, ole boy. I've waited too long for my plans to be destroyed by the likes of you," hissed the jack-o'-lantern as Carl's eyes closed for the last time. The jack-o'-lantern flung Carl's shriveled corpse against the wall, turning his attention toward Margie.

As he turned, he noticed something familiar sticking out of Margie's backpack atop her dresser. It was the spell book belonging to the Witch of Willow Branch. He looked from the book to the girl on the bed, and a soft glow came to his expression.

"Impossible! How is it possible, Marguarette, that after all of these years, you could look so youthful?" The jack-o'-lantern grew solemn. "I look different now. Shouldn't you? Is this more of your magic spells at work? Or is this really you at all? I must find out."

The jack-o'-lantern had been transformed by the witch who had possessed this spell book many years ago. Now the creature wondered if she could change him back. He had had enough. He hated hiding from the devil; he hated running. He hated wandering the netherworld without purpose. He had waited a long time for this moment, and he wanted revenge for all he had suffered. This witch and her spell book could give him everything.

Gus and Molly arrived at Margie's house on the run, gasping for air, and what they saw filled them with dread. Carl's truck was in the driveway, and the front door stood wide open. They rushed to the door and listened. They heard a loud bang, like something hitting a wall, deeper inside the house. Curious, they crept inward. The house was trashed; they dodged broken bottles and overturned furniture until they reached the hallway. They saw that the door to Margie's room looked like it had been ripped from its hinges.

Gus and Molly inched toward her doorway, afraid of what they might find. Grandma Bertie had told them Margie and her stepfather did not get along and that Margie would stay with her when it got too bad. Grandma Bertie could not tolerate abusive alcoholics. She would become enraged when discussing Carl and alcoholics like him. She never explained to them why she felt so strongly, and they never did ask. They both froze in their tracks at what they saw.

The jack-o'-lantern had Margie in his arms. With her backpack over his shoulder and one leg through her open window, the jack-o'-lantern ducked his head through. As he did, he looked back over his shoulder. Flame flared from his eyes when he recognized Gus. Fear and fury filled them both as they stared at each other. Margie began to wake in the creature's arms.

The jack-o'-lantern sprinted away as Margie cried out, "Help me, Gus! Help me!" Margie's voice faded in the distance as Gus ran to the window. He had one leg out ready to follow when Molly pulled him back inside.

"What are you doing?" he roared.

Molly pointed toward the opposite wall. "Saving your life. I think that might be Carl," Molly said, pointing at the withered corpse that resembled a skeleton rolled in Saran Wrap.

"I'm calling the police. We have a murder to report," she said as she fished her phone from her front pocket to dial 911.

"And don't forget to mention a kidnap—," Gus began, but something in Margie's closet caught his attention. "Look at this," he said, holding up a pair of old black work boots that had to be too big for Margie. Molly also pointed out the dirt in a pot in the closet.

"I think we've found our garden thief." She could tell by his expression that Gus wasn't following. "The missing dirt, the heel print (these boots must be Carl's because they are a size 10½), the appearance of the jack-o'-lantern, and your nightmares. Gus, it all adds up. Margie was the one who brought the jack-o'-lantern back."

"But how did it survive? And why would she do such a thing? It makes no sense," Gus huffed, still frustrated that Molly did not let him go after Margie. "If he hurts her…" Gus dropped his head into his hands, trying to hold back his tears. Molly put her arms around her brother and stroked his back as the sirens grew louder.

Red flashing lights from three Willow Branch police cars greeted Grandma Bertie as she parked her red-and-white Ford truck across the street from the single-story brick ranch of Carl Hughes. She got out and walked across the street toward the house. She saw the kids sitting on the front porch talking to one of the officers.

"Are you kids all right? Where's Margie?" Grandma Bertie asked with a worried look upon her face. They both jumped up and gave her a big hug.

"Yeah, we're okay. Margie was taken," Gus said with a strange look on his face as if he was trying to speak with his eyes. Grandma Bertie looked at Molly for an explanation, but she shook her head as if to say "Not now."

"Chief O'Reilly, can I take them home now?" Bertie asked. The officer nodded.

"I have their statements, and if we need anything further, we will be in touch." He looked at Gus and Molly. "Thanks again, kids, for reporting this as soon as you did. It will help us to find your friend. Here's my card. If you have anything else you remember, please call us."

11

They all nodded at the chief of police as they walked toward Grandma Bertie's truck. They rode in silence for a while. Gus looked back over his shoulder then spun back around and spoke.

"Grandma, the jack-o'-lantern is back, and he took Margie." Her eyes bulged in shock. She looked at Molly for confirmation; she nodded in agreement with Gus's story.

"But how?" Grandma Bertie blankly asked.

"*Stop the truck!*" Gus screamed, and Grandma Bertie hit the brakes. The tires screeched to a halt in front of a house with a lawn that looked like it had been neglected for months.

"Gus, what on earth?" Grandma Bertie scolded.

"Sorry," Gus apologized. "This is it! This is the house from my dream. Let me out!" Confused and intrigued by Gus's behavior, Molly slid out of the truck first, and they followed Gus toward the house. They weaved through the tall grass to the backyard, where a small shattered greenhouse stood with its open doors hanging off the hinges. Inside, they saw footprints similar to the one Mr. Grogan found in Grandma Bertie's garden.

Molly looked at Gus. "They are the same."

"What is going on, you two? What is the same?" Grandma Bertie protested. Molly stood and tried to explain.

"A few days ago, Mr. Grogan found a partial footprint next to a hole in your garden where someone had taken some of your dirt."

"Now who would do a thing like that?" Grandma Bertie asked. Gus climbed the backyard fence, looked left and right to get his bearings, and jumped back to the ground. Molly watched as she continued.

"Today, in Margie's closet, we found a pair of boots the same size and with the same tread as the print Mr. Grogan found. We also found vines similar to these in a broken terrarium in Margie's closet. And dirt was all over the closet floor." She looked at Gus for support, but he was focused on something else. Molly continued.

"We believe Margie took soil from your garden so she could restore the sickly vine that she must've found here. She repotted it in a dome with full-spectrum lighting in her closet. Gus?"

Molly looked to Gus for the rest of the story. Gus slowly turned to face them both.

"Sorry. It's just that… I saw all of this," Gus said, spinning around, motioning with his hands at everything around him. "Everything you see here, I saw in my dream. This is where the jack-o'-lantern chased me and was obliterated by the train. This is the place!"

"What happened in your dream, Gus? Tell me everything you can remember," Grandma Bertie said.

Gus sat Indian style; Grandma Bertie and Molly followed his lead. Gus surveyed his surroundings. The shattered greenhouse in the back, the sea of uncut grass waving in the breeze, and the mossy smell of earth beneath him opened up the memories locked away in the closets of his mind. He finally began to recall his dreams.

"Well," he began, "I remember running for a touchdown. I had just crossed the twenty-yard line heading into the end zone when my legs turned to jelly and a thick fog appeared from nowhere in front of me. I could not see anything, not even my feet below me. I wanted to score so badly. I kept running, hoping the fog wouldn't keep the refs from seeing when I entered the end zone. But I never scored. Instead, I ran into a wall—not the wall of the stadium but a backyard fence. I climbed to the top of the fence and heard a familiar, evil-sounding voice. The fog cleared, and I was face-to-face with the jack-o'-lantern!"

Gus was reliving the whole nightmare. Molly and Grandma Bertie saw the horror in his eyes, but they didn't say a word. They feared they would interrupt his vision. They listened and watched in awe.

"I dropped to the ground and ran so hard, so fast that my side hurt. I couldn't breathe. It came after me. It chased me through the neighborhood, and I found myself on the railroad tracks like before. I saw the steeple of the church, and then I fell. It was standing over me. I thought it was going to get me, but a light was shining behind the jack-o'-lantern. I jumped into the ditch as a train smashed the jack-o'-lantern." Gus stopped to catch his breath.

"Gooey pieces of pumpkin flew everywhere. I swallowed a slimy seed, I think." Grandma Bertie gasped. Molly nearly jumped out of her skin, startled by her grandmother's response. Molly watched Grandma Bertie become shaken by Gus's nightmare, especially about the seed he had swallowed.

"You swallowed a seed of that monster?" Bertie asked.

"Yeah, I think so. It tasted awful."

"Oh dear, oh dear," Bertie cried out. "Oh dear, oh dear, oh dear." Gus freaked.

"Is that bad?" Gus squeaked.

"Grandma, please! Tell us what is wrong!" Molly begged.

Grandma Bertie saw the horror on the kids' faces and snapped out of her stupor.

"Oh, it's nothing. Really, I just can't stand the thought of swallowing slimy pumpkin seeds. It gives me the willies." She shuddered.

"Me too!" Gus roared. "Disgusting! But I do love them cooked with butter and—"

"Gus!" Molly cut him off from rambling any further. She wasn't sure she believed Grandma's dismissive answer, but she was ready to hear more of Gus's nightmare stories. "Is that it, or do you have more to tell us?" Molly asked with pinched lips.

"About what?" Gus asked. Molly blew her top.

"Gus! Your dreams! *Focus*," she groaned.

"Oh. Yeah, right. Sorry." Gus continued. "So I was walking home and saw this place," he said, looking around where they sat.

"It seemed to draw me in, and I saw this pathway through the tall grass." He motioned with his hand at the dirt where they sat. "So I followed it. And I saw him! I saw them—hundreds of them!" Gus's eyes bulged in fear.

"You saw who, Gus?" Grandma calmly asked.

Gus spoke as if he had not heard Grandma Bertie's question. "They are climbing up out of the ground. They are all looking at me! They are coming for me!"

"Who is, Gus? Who is coming for you?" Molly yelled.

"The jack-o'-lantern and his pumpkin army are after me! He said he is going to kill me!" Gus gasped for air as his vision vanished as quickly as it had appeared. Molly put her arms around her brother's shoulders, trying to stop him from shaking. Grandma Bertie was in deep thought. Molly intently watched her, observing her facial expressions. She could almost see Grandma Bertie's mind in motion.

"Is that all, dear?" Bertie asked, breaking a long silence.

Gus nodded, still shaking. "That's it for that dream anyway. I don't want to remember any more right now."

"Let's get you kids home, and we can talk about it later," Bertie said. They hopped back in Grandma's truck and headed home, which was just around the corner.

12

At the base of a large beech-tree deep in the woods, a glowing fire warmed Margie as she slept. Satisfied with his work, the jack-o'-lantern disappeared into the darkness with Margie's backpack on its shoulder. He was going to stop in on an old friend.

A guard at the gates of hell relayed a message to his master.

"My Prince," the servant whispered into the devil's ear, "we have a visitor, and he wants to speak with you."

The Prince's brow rose with curiosity, and then he smiled. "Then by all means, let him in," said the devil. "It isn't every day someone *asks* to see me." The devil did not recognize Jack, but he did recognize the glow within the jack-o'-lantern's skull. Satan eyed his strange visitor; he had never before seen a walking, talking jack-o'-lantern.

"Who would request an audience with me here, the last place any living person would choose to be?" The Prince of Darkness quizzed.

"I do not qualify for living at present. My name is Jack. You do not recognize me because a witch has hidden me from you for hundreds of years." The jack-o'-lantern smirked.

"State your purpose! I have no patience for riddles or use for talking vegetables," the devil growled.

"I wish to make a deal with you," Jack said with a mischievous grin.

"You wish to make a deal? With me?" The devil paused. "Your name is Jack, you say? Hmmm." Satan began to piece the puzzle together. "Oh yes. Yes, I remember you now. This explains the familiar glow within your skull. Yes, I have waited a long time for this moment for my revenge to be complete." The devil glared at Jack. "Take him!" Two menacing demons standing as guards moved closer to Jack. Jack quickly got to his purpose.

"I have something that belongs to you, and I believe you want it back."

"And what do you think I am doing? When my servants rip your skull open, I will have what you stole from me," the devil bellowed.

"Not that. This!" Jack held up the thick leather-bound spell book taken from Margie's backpack.

The devil raised his hand, and the demons stopped. He looked at Jack.

"Where did you get that?" Smoke spewed from the brimstone floor; the rotten-egg smell of sulfur surrounded the devil as he stood up from his throne.

"I found a young witch with this book. She brought me once again to this form," Jack said.

The devil stopped in his tracks halfway toward Jack, raised his gaze from the floor, and peered into Jack's eyes. Then he turned back around after taking a closer look at the book.

"This was mine, but I gave it as a gift. It can only be returned to me by her with a sacrifice of flesh and blood. *You* can perform neither and are of no use to me," the devil shouted. With a wave of his hand, the demon henchmen grabbed Jack.

"Wait! Listen to me! I have a plan that will remedy all of that and benefit both of us. Please, listen to me," Jack pleaded.

The devil dropped his hand, and his henchmen stopped. The devil spun around upon his throne, looking at Jack with eyes that would have pierced any mortal soul. Jack quickly spoke of his plan. When he finished, he stared at the devil for a response. The devil took his time surveying every possible scenario before he spoke.

"And what is it you wish in return?" The devil asked, leaning down toward Jack.

"I don't ever want to die." Jack grinned.

The devil grimaced, and his wry smile blossomed. "As you wish," the devil hissed. His henchmen dropped Jack to the sulfuric floor.

Jack turned and ran out of sight. With a twitch of his devilish hand, Satan called forth the night hag, Mara.

"Monitor this boy you found. His connection to this creature is strong, and he will betray the jack-o'-lantern's true plans. The witch was very cunning in hiding Jack from me in this form, but I will not be fooled again. The boy's dreams will betray Jack, and at long last, I will finally have my revenge, once and for all. There must be no mistakes," the devil growled.

Mara vanished into the night.

13

Molly was visibly upset with Gus. Since getting into Grandma Bertie's truck, he seemed to get his second wind for telling his dreams—dreams of running naked in the school halls and scoring touchdowns naked. In another story, a naked Gus rescued a girl imprisoned in an underground city guarded by giant cockroaches.

Gus observed his sister's red face. She was about to explode, so he reluctantly returned to retelling his dreaded nightmares of the jack-o'-lantern.

"There was another with the jack-o'-lantern in it, but I don't want to tell it," Gus said as he stared at his feet dangling beneath the bench seat of the Ford.

"Gus, I know this is difficult for you, but I believe your dreams may help us find Margie. Please try for her," Grandma Bertie encouraged.

Gus took a deep cleansing breath. "Awright. For Margie," Gus replied, glancing at Grandma Bertie and his sister. "I am walking along a dirt path. It has moss running up the middle of it and trees with large trunks along the edges. I am lost. I do not know where I am or where I am going, but I keep moving. There is fog again, and it is thick, like walking in the clouds. Then I hear a girl screaming, 'Let me go! Let me go. I won't do it!' I run toward the screams, and then I stop. I am petrified by what I hear next."

"Go on, dear," Grandma Bertie said.

"I hear another voice—his voice, the voice of the jack-o'-lantern. He tells the girl if she doesn't do as he says, then she will never see her mother again." Molly gently rubs her brother's back, silently encouraging him to continue.

"Then I saw a light, and I felt safe, and I was able to move again, but then I realized the feeling couldn't be trusted. It was the glow of the jack-o'-lantern towering above me. 'Jack's back, little boy, and it is time to pull you up by the roots!' he screamed at me. I ran back down the path as fast as I could until I heard the girl calling for help again. 'Help me! Please, somebody help me!' And then I woke up with her sitting on my chest," Gus said, pointing at Molly.

"Who? Who was sittin' on your chest, Gus?" Grandma Bertie exploded, still watching the road.

Gus looked at her as if she had lost her mind. "Molly was, Grandma."

"Oh," Bertie said, which wasn't sufficient for Molly.

"Who did you think was sitting on his chest, Grandma?" Molly asked with peaked curiosity.

"Oh I don't know, dear. I jus' got caught up in his story. That's all," Bertie said, forcing a smile as she pulled into the Johnson driveway. Molly felt certain that Grandma Bertie wasn't telling them everything.

"You two go pack enough to stay the week, and I'll see you in a little bit," Grandma Bertie said with a smile. She backed out of the drive and pulled away. Molly walked to the edge of the road, looking at the truck as it sped away.

"What are you doin'?" Gus asked.

"Just wondering what she is up to. Her house is in the opposite direction," Molly said in deep thought.

"So?" Gus jabbed. "You worry too much. Come on. Let's get packed."

––––––––––––

Jack's patience with the witch's method of protecting him as a pumpkin all these years was finally paying off. He had stumbled onto a master plan that would give him eternal life, cheating death once again and for all time. He was again using the devil against his knowledge and will. Jack had to be patient a little longer while taking care of his greatest ally and pawn.

The jack-o'-lantern scooped up the sleeping girl, kicked dirt on the smoldering coals of the campfire, and marched out of the woods. He wanted Margie to volunteer to help him in his devilish plan or he needed to coerce her. But for the moment, he needed to keep her alive and safe. He could do none of this on his own.

He stopped. He was ready to execute the first portion of his plan. He laid the girl down and reached into her backpack, pulling out her school notebook. To the best of his third grade education, he scratched out a message to Margie.

To Marguarette, the Witch of Willow Branch

I need your help, my dear. You aided me once, and I am in need again. I know what your heart desires. I can help you. Find the spell that will bring her back. Test it on me, and I will help you succeed. Soon you will be with her forever. When you are ready, you'll know where to find me.

Jack

The jack-o'-lantern stuffed the note inside the backpack as lights shone from the distance toward him and the girl. He disappeared in the roadside brush as Grandma Bertie's truck sped down the road.

Bertie had spent the last two hours searching for Margie. She went to the woods, the Shelter Tree, the school, her home, and back to the Shelter Tree. *Where is Margie? Where is he keepin' her?*

Bertie was deep in thought. She was on autopilot. Then suddenly, something in the road commanded her attention. It was too big to be a possum or a raccoon. Bertie slammed on the brakes, and her truck screeched to a halt six inches from the heap in the road—six inches from running over her precious Margie.

Margie moved slowly and moaned as the effects of the jack-o'-lantern's needle began to wear off. Bertie was overcome by emotion. She picked up Margie and gently placed her in the cab of her truck. Bertie threw Margie's heavy bag in the back and headed home.

14

The Ford slid to a stop in Bertie's gravel drive. She yelled for help.

"Steven! I found her! I found her!" Steven burst out of the front door and ran to Bertie. "She was lying in the middle of the road. She must have escaped and collapsed onto the road. She is cold, Steven."

"I'll take her. You go in and fix her a hot bath," Steven said calmly.

Bertie ran for the house. She started the bath, warmed up some of her cure-all chicken noodle soup, and made peanut butter and jelly sandwiches, slicing them into wedges.

Margie was still in a fog; she hadn't said a word. She was exhausted even after sleeping all day. She ate ravenously while she soaked in a soothing hot bath. Bertie tucked her in for the night an hour later in the newly renovated spare bedroom.

Since Margie's mother's death, Bertie had been hoping for the day Margie would come to permanently live with her. She only wished the circumstances were different. She never liked Carl, Margie's stepfather. After marrying Melinda, he became a vile man, especially toward Margie. He forced Melinda to sell the old farmhouse that she had purchased from Bertie to help him pay off his old gambling debts and live in a small ranch home down the same street. But she would not have wished his fate on anyone.

Steven Grogan poked his head around the screened front door, not wanting to disturb Bertie. She appeared to be focused elsewhere as she washed the evening's dishes. She looked up from the foamy water and stared out the window with a faraway look in her eye. Steven placed his large warm hand on her shoulder.

"You look like you are in deep thought. Mind sharing?" Steven grinned.

"She's home now, Steven. She is finally home." Bertie began to cry. Steven put his arms around her and held her tight. He knew how much Margie meant to her. He knew Bertie's emotions stretched further back than her two-hour search for Margie. Bertie had waited years for this moment. Finally, Margie was here, and Steven knew that Margie came with the package. He had to help raise a child if he wanted to marry Bertie.

"Bertie," he whispered, "the court will not allow her to stay here unless you are married." Her face grew grim at the thought. But before she could speak, he gently placed his large finger over her mouth.

"Bertie, will you marry me?"

Bertie's mad face faded; her tears flowed freely. Looking in Steven's eyes, she managed to whisper, "Yes!" Steven softly hugged and kissed her as she cried even harder.

Suddenly, headlights appeared in the driveway. "Well, looks like the kids are here," Steven said. Bertie wiped her face, smiling up at him again.

"Yes, they are. It's going to be a great week having them all to myself." He looked at her over the rims of his spectacles under raised eyebrows. She got the message. "*We* have them all to *ourselves!*" Bertie smiled. "I love you, Steven."

He grinned warmly. "I love you, Bertie."

Just then, the kids crashed through the front door. "Beat yah." Molly huffed.

"No, you didn't. You cheated. You got out of the van before I did. That's not fair," Gus whined.

"You were saying?" Steven joked. Bertie rolled her eyes, smiling.

Janice Johnson came through the front door dressed in old sweats and flip-flops, looking frazzled and forced a smile. "They're all yours!" she exhaled. "They've been at each other's throat since you dropped them off. I gotta go pack so that I can leave home before midnight. I should be able to get to Minnesota by tomorrow night if I drive straight through, resting along the way, of course. My first interview isn't scheduled until 11:00 a.m.

Friday." She hugged Gus while avoiding Bertie's glare of concern about the trip.

They had already had a very long discussion about Janice driving to Minnesota instead of Bertie paying for a flight. Janice wanted to save money. More importantly, she wanted to cut her dependency on Bertie. Janice felt the need to be the sole provider for her family. While Bertie understood, she didn't like not being allowed to help when she saw a need.

Janice was heading to Minnesota for a series of job interviews. She had been searching for some time. This opportunity looked too good to be true with nearly twice the salary she needed, so she was very excited. She was ready for a new challenge—a new adventure—even if it meant moving her family far from home. The kids were not so excited.

"I'm only a phone call away. You'll be fine." Janice reassured Molly with a hug. "Wish me luck," she said as she headed out the door.

"Good luck!" Everyone cheered as Janice pulled away in her run-down minivan. Grandma Bertie put her arms around Gus and Molly as they made their way down the hall to the guest room she just converted from a junk room.

"I have another surprise for you," she said, opening the bedroom door. "I found Margie!"

Their eyes blossomed in disbelieving joy.

15

Steven brought in Margie's backpack along with two heavy trash bags of clothes from the back of Bertie's truck. With full hands, he stopped at the bedroom door and watched the gleam in Bertie's eyes.

Bertie watched her kids enjoy one another's company. They were safe, and she was full of joy—for the first time in years. She turned her eyes toward the door, glanced at Steven, and began to cry.

Molly was thrilled that Margie was back, but something alarmed her. She tapped Grandma Bertie on the shoulder and whispered in her ear.

"Grandma, can I talk to you privately?"

Bertie had an inquisitive look on her face. "Sure, dear, sure," Bertie whispered. Turning around, she saw Gus and Margie hugging. She hated to break up their moment, but it had been a long day.

"Come on, let's let Margie get some rest. She's had a very rough day."

Gus whined in rebellion but to no avail. At the door, Bertie turned, took a deep sigh, blew Margie a kiss, and said good night.

"Now then," Bertie said with hands on Gus and Molly as they headed toward the kitchen, "is it all right if Gus listens in or did you mean the two of us alone, Molly?"

"No, Gus is fine. I just didn't want to discuss this in front of Margie. She's had too much drama for one lifetime let alone one day." They sat down at the kitchen table.

Steven knew he had no part in this conversation. "I think I'll head home and let you talk. See you in the mornin'," he said as he kissed Bertie good-bye.

Bertie watched him leave and gradually turned her attention to Gus and Molly, who rolled their eyes.

"What?" Bertie protested. Gus and Molly giggled.

"Oh nothing," Molly said. "We're just glad to see you are happy again."

Bertie smiled and nodded.

"Now, what is it ya need to talk about? It is gettin' late, ya know."

"Grandma, the last time we saw Margie, she was being abducted by the jack-o'-lantern. How did she escape and get here? How did the jack-o'-lantern return, and why does it exist?"

Gus looked at Molly in amazement. It was like she had read his mind. He turned his attention to Grandma in anticipation of her answers.

Bertie sat back in her chair to consider Molly's questions. She stared out the sliding glass door to the wooded area that used to be her special garden.

Bertie considered giving them a brief, aloof response with no real answers because she was tired. It was late, and she was ready for bed. But when she saw genuine concern on their faces, she decided to open the door of truth a little wider.

"Well, you remember the story of Billy Gipson and the curse of the jack-o'-lantern that I told you about? Well, I believe it started long before that in Ireland." Bertie paused for a moment, still struggling with revealing the past to the kids. Their intense looks encouraged her to continue her journey back in time. She told them the story of Stingy Jack and his poor wife, Lady Marguarette.

"It was Lady Marguarette's daughter who Willow Branch residents mistook for a witch. They sent this poor innocent girl to the Salem witch trials—to her doom.

"When Lady Marguarette found out, she lost herself to fear, anger, rage, and hate. The townspeople were wrong in accusing her innocent daughter, so she made sure they paid the price. Marguarette *was* a peaceful witch—that is, until they stole her daughter away to her death.

"Death for accused witches included public ridicule and water torture to drag out a confession followed by burning at the stake to kill the evil spirits.

"The innocent child's mother, Lady Marguarette, swore: 'This town will now and forevermore know what a witch is capable of and that *I* am the *real* Witch of Willow Branch!' In her grief and rage, she opened a forbidden door to the grave and beyond to exact her revenge upon the town.

"She cursed the ground so it would not yield crops," Bertie continued. "Many starved, and others lost their farms and had to move away. Those who managed to survive suffered even more.

"The witch was not satisfied until all suffered as she did. She used a curse to summon someone from the grave. He was to spread wrath in retaliation for the unjust death of her daughter. She gave this lost soul a temporary body and unleashed him upon the town, terrorizing those who had survived the famine."

Gus and Molly were on the edge of their seats. They were shocked but eager to hear more.

"How do you know all of this, Grandma?" Molly inquired as Bertie fumbled for the right words.

"Uh...well... Uh, it's the history of Willow Branch, and I became aware of it when I came to Willow Branch a long time ago. Shall I continue?"

A satisfied Molly nodded.

"Lady Marguarette, the Witch of Willow Branch, was angry and arrogant," Bertie continued. "She believed she commanded and controlled the powerful magic she had learned. But she was only a pawn—a pawn of the devil!"

Gus and Molly gasped at the thought. Suddenly they were no longer tired. Bertie looked grim as she continued.

"The witch had been used to unwittingly open a forbidden spiritual path so that the devil could circumvent an ancient curse that had been cast upon him," Grandma said. "The curse had protected mankind from his direct attacks, but a few loopholes exist, allowing him free reign on humanity. Only an all-powerful spell could close this door tightly. The devil had access to harm the townspeople through the agent the witch had chosen, bypassing the original curse that was placed on the devil's powers.

"The Devil had planned for the agent of destruction. The witch was just a pawn. She was never in control."

Molly interrupted, "The jack-o'-lantern was the agent?"

Bertie closed her eyes and nodded. "The witch used a powerful spell from the book given to her by the devil. A door opened, bringing Jack back as the jack-o'-lantern. He mercilessly attacked the town, burning houses and businesses with no regard for their occupants.

"The witch saw the error of her anger and rage. She helplessly tried to stop the jack-o'-lantern, but he was determined to carry out his own revenge upon the living, which ultimately pleased the devil.

"Once Willow Branch was destroyed, the jack-o'-lantern was bound to destroy every town on the way to Salem and beyond.

"Guilt kept the Witch from allowing the wrath to spill beyond Willow Branch. She devised a plan. The jack-o'-lantern returned daily to a small plot of soil that was enhanced by the witch and not cursed like the rest of Willow Branch. There he hid from the sun to replenish his killing strength.

"The jack-o'-lantern sank into the bed of soil that day," Bertie tensely continued. "Noticing something just below the surface, he reached down and lifted the foreign piece. At once, his limbs were frozen. In his hand was a silver cross that rendered the jack-o'-lantern helpless.

"The witch seized the moment, severing the head and burning the remains. That ended the devil's reign of terror until poor Billy Gipson unwittingly called the curse of the jack-o'-lantern back into power many years later." Grandma Bertie sighed in relief as she finished the story.

"And then, Mom and Gus brought the jack-o'-lantern back again when he picked the pumpkin from your patch in September even after he had heard the story that you told us as a warning and she carved it!" Molly had a look of stone, still angry at her brother's stupidity and deep in thought. "But, Grandma, we saw it destroyed," she said at last. "How then has it returned?"

"I do not know, child," Bertie replied. *But,* she thought, *I wonder if Gus's dreams may not hold a clue or two.*

"Grandma," Molly began, "how did Margie escape from the jack-o'-lantern when no one else could all those years ago?"

"I don't know, dear. I found her out cold in the middle of the street just a few yards up the road."

"Seems like a strange place to take a nap," Gus said.

Molly glared at him for his lack of compassion. But then she agreed with him. "What if Margie did not escape?" Molly inquired as the wheels in her keen mind spun at full steam. "What if she was placed there to be discovered?"

"That's crazy. Did you really just say that?" Gus scowled.

"Well, I'm glad it happened, if it did happen as you suggest," Grandma Bertie replied. "I don't care why or how. She's back, and that's all that matters now.

"But there is something we must do. We must find the jack-o'-lantern and end this curse by closing the door that was opened by the Witch of Willow Branch all those years ago. We must undo this terrible evil, and we must do it before more innocent people die."

"What do you mean, Grandma?" Gus croaked.

"As long as the jack-o'-lantern exists, the door remains open," Bertie explained. "On behalf of the devil, more agents will pass through the door, wielding power and destruction over the world. For every evil spirit that crosses the grave and enters the present, one soul from the present must be sent back as payment."

"Grandma, you mean more spirits could come and more people could die?" Molly gasped.

"No, dear. More *are* coming. More *will* die."

"But, Grandma," Gus pleaded, "we destroyed the jack-o'-lantern before he was able to kill anyone the last time."

Bertie looked at him blankly. "I know. That's what's been troublin' me. It must fulfill the payment of the curse or it will perish. And it craves life above all. That's why I am so glad Margie is safe. She could have—should have been taken. Carl took the place of your mom as far as the curse was concerned, but another should have been needed for its return. We must find the jack-o'-lantern before it's too late."

16

In the closet of Margie's former bedroom sat the plant in the special soil. Its shimmering leaves violently shook. Rising from the pot was an orange orb—a pumpkin with eyes as black as coal. Once it broke the surface, green vines gripped the sides of the pot's rim and pulled its sinewy body out of the pot.

The unnatural creature stepped forward and stretched as another head came to the surface and pulled itself free of the pot. Taking the pot of soil, they stepped through the open window and disappeared into the night as quickly as they had appeared.

17

Janice Johnson had finished packing and showering. She was ready to head for Minnesota in a rental car. She decided her van was unfit for the trip, so Rent-A-Ride delivered a black Dodge Charger to her door.

She sped off through the neighborhood past Bertie's house onto the back road that wrapped around the hills of Willow Branch Forest.

Winding Hill Road was the shortest path to the freeway. Her tires squealed as she rounded every curve faster than she should. She was in a hurry, and the Charger had plenty of horsepower.

Janice's heart pounded to the beat of the blaring music. The radio screen read Heavy Metal/Metallica/Enter Sandman.

> Exit light
> Enter night
> Grain of sand

Janice looked down to change the station. The vibrations were making her more nervous than her speed.

Her right-side tires caught the gravel from the roadside, kicking up a cloud of dust that jerked her attention from the radio back to the road. She overcorrected with a hard left turn, nearly running off the left ledge of the road and down the sheer face of the cliff.

Janice corrected back to the right, finally settling back on her side of the road just as a pickup truck whizzed past.

Out of the corner of her eye she saw *it*.

Janice slammed on the brakes. The tires screamed as she steered through a gravel-strewn cloud into a convenience-store lot where two rusty gas pumps sat.

> Off to never-never land

Janice quickly turned off the car to run inside for a fountain soda for the road.

She pushed the door open and heard the same song pounding the air through the stores speaker system. Behind the cash register at the front counter, sat a clerk who was reading, leaning back on a chair, balancing on its rear two legs with his feet crossed.

Janice asked for the location of the fountain soda machine. The teen-aged boy nonchalantly pointed to the rear of the store without looking up from his comic book. Janice found the soda machine and soon headed to the register to pay.

> Grippin' your pillow tight
> Exit light
> Enter night

"What's with this music? Doesn't it make you want to kill somebody?" she asked the pimply faced clerk behind the counter.

His eyes looked up from under his baseball cap, but his body did not flinch. "Eighty-nine cents," he said with little interest.

Manners? They must be scraping the bottom of the barrel for employees. He could have said, "Did you find everything okay, ma'am?" or "Good evening, ma'am." What's this generation coming to? She mined her purse for correct change.

The clerk had his own thoughts: *Come on, lady. You are holdin' up my literary endeavors! Finally! Why are old people so clueless?* He returned to reading before she could grab her soda. Janice shot him a look, shook her head, and ran back to her car. She placed the soda in the center console and took a deep breath. The silence in the car was calming.

"Okay, here we go," she said aloud. She adjusted the rearview mirror so she could back out of the parking space. She turned the key, and the Hemi engine roared to life.

> Take my hand
> Off to never-never land

The volume of the song startled her; she frantically searched for the volume control.

Something in the rearview mirror caught her attention. Janice looked up and saw glowing triangular eyes glaring back at her. She turned to scream, but as the song faded, everything in her world turned black as she slid down the seat. She looked up into the face of the jack-o'-lantern once more.

"Here we go indeed," the jack-o'-lantern's raspy voice growled from the backseat. Its gnarled hand of vine reached for her as the song ended.

> Take my hand
> Off to never-never land
> Off to never-never land
> Off to never-never land

REVENGE OF THE JACK-O'-LANTERN AND THE WITCH OF WILLOW BRANCH

PROLOGUE

Massachusetts, 1862

Two black-maned draft horses reared their thick-feathered hooves to a stop as the driver of the modest carriage pulled the reins, halting at the signpost on the outskirts of town. White clouds billowed from the horses' nostrils as grey clouds hovered above. It was a brisk morning as the carriage suddenly stopped; Reverend Michael O'Reilly woke with a chill as the driver opened the carriage door.

"You can walk from here," the bearded driver said gruffly. The reverend looked aghast at the man, his mind not yet alert from his deep sleep.

"Why have we stopped?" the reverend asked.

"This is as fer as I go. Tha town is cursed. Killin' witches an all."

Reverend O'Reilly could see the fear in the man's face as he looked wearily at the distant town.

"I'll be goin' no ferther. Thank you. It is a short walk from here. The courthouse is on yer right."

The reverend assessed the man for a superstitious fool but smiled, thanked him, and said a prayer for his soul as he headed into town down a muddy dirt road.

"Good luck to ya, revren'!" the driver shouted as he guided his stout horses back onto the road heading away from town.

Reverend O'Reilly turned and waved good-bye. Turning around again, he passed the town sign that read Salem.

The damp, cold, October air chilled the girl huddling in the corner of a stone room of the town's jail. A filthy cattle stall would have been a more pleasant place to lay one's head. The barred window provided a slice of freshened air to that of the stench of human waste and vomit. The redheaded girl shook uncontrollably, sitting on a thin layer of straw in her corner of the overcrowded cell.

Lilly Morgan had been in Salem for three days, and for three days it had rained. The streets were as muddy as the justice being served by the local magistrate. She had been taken from her home in Willow Branch and accused of the popular crime of the times—witchcraft.

Lilly had been publically humiliated, chastised by the church leaders, spit upon, cursed, and riddled with rotten vegetables at the hands of vengeful onlookers. Yet at this moment, she counted herself among the lucky ones. She had survived where others had not.

The previous day, she and seven other women accused of witchcraft had been dunked headfirst one at a time into a drum of water with their hands tied behind them. They were pulled up coughing and gasping for air and forced to admit their guilt.

"Do you confess to these crimes?" A red-faced bishop yelled in Lilly's ear, shaking his fist before her face. "Admit that you are indeed a witch, a child of Satan himself, and your misery shall end. *Do you confess?*" screamed Bishop Van Buren, exciting the crowd, which hurled insults at those on the stage.

One by one, all eight accused suffered, gagging, choking, and gasping for air, for life. Five had confessed to the charges brought against them and were sent back wet to the cold, stinking jail cell to await trial. The remaining three unrelenting souls drowned before they would confess. All three were Christians, believers in Christ, and considered it blasphemy to confess to being a child of Satan. The five that had confessed were not as strong in their faith.

Heavy footsteps stopped behind the thick wooden cell door. The rusted hinges creaked as the door opened. An officer of the court stepped to the doorway but refused to set foot inside. The sickening odor nearly made him wretch. Breathing through his mouth, he held a scroll in his hands and called forth those to appear before the people.

Melinda James
Contessa Stewart
Ruby Holland
Lilly Morgan
Wilma Schimdt

"Follow me and take your stand before the charges set against you." The court officer clicked his heels and spun around, leading them all down a long dark stone-block corridor that opened into a large, spacious room of dark wood with a high balcony full of jeering onlookers. They took their place on the stage facing the crowded courtroom.

It was a room that doubled as the town theatre, which some thought was appropriate that it was also where the town's justice was presented.

Some felt that the actions of the church leaders and the town officials were nothing more than an act in a play to win the applause of the whimsical audience. They were clearly more concerned with their reviews or reelection status than any truth or justice. They were often accused of fear mongering and power brokering to gain support or a forced following.

The trials against witchcraft served both purposes as sightings and accusations from superstitious patrons gave the leadership of the church and town an opportunity to gain support as they came to the aid and rescue of a town obviously under attack by supernatural forces.

The women huddled onstage, facing a packed house. Bishop Van Buren stood facing the women from a podium on the far side of the room; the sun shone through the large glass windows, cloaking him in a superficial aura of majesty. The newly appointed public defender, Jonathon Bodkins, was given the task of counsel for the accused; he stood at the front of the room next to the accused women.

Bishop Van Buren hammered his gavel on the podium, where he stood and opened the trial with his list of accusations and evidences against each woman.

Melinda Jones, Contessa Stewart, and Ruby Holland were accused of mocking the minister and causing a disruption during another church service and also with meeting in secret in the woods and dancing by firelight, which was commonly known to be a ritual of the craft for communicating with the dead. They refused the counsel of young Mr. Bodkins on the basis that they were unsure they wanted to trust their lives to a man that it was questionable whether he had yet reached puberty.

They denied all charges and were swiftly sentenced.

Wilma Schmidt confessed to animal sacrifice, devil worship, and possessing a melancholy spirit. They should have added speaking in tongues because poor Ms. Schmidt had only recently arrived from her native country of Germany two months prior to her arrest. She spoke only German; she had no idea what was being said or what was happening to her.

Outsiders were reserved for last. Lilly Morgan, a scared child, only thirteen years old, faced the accusations brought against her. Church leaders from Willow Branch had her brought to Salem for trial as a witch.

Reverend O'Reilly had come on behalf of her mother, after waiting two days for Lady Marguarette Morgan to return to Willow Branch from a short trip to neighboring towns, selling her herbs as their only means of support. When she had not arrived, he left in hopes of rescuing Lilly with his testimony of her character in the face of these false charges.

He knew that she was a sweet, innocent young girl full of love and joy. She was forever smiling; she embodied happiness. Reverend O'Reilly joined Mr. Bodkins at the front of the theatre.

"Lilly Morgan, you have confessed to being an artisan of witchcraft. These being the accusations brought against you as follows: frequent unchaperoned walks into the woods, chanting even in public places, carrying herbs from the woods on several occasions, all confirmed activities of witchcraft. What is your defense to these evidences laid before you?" Bishop Van Buren said, glaring up at her from his notes, waiting for a response from her defense.

Reverend O'Reilly nudged Mr. Bodkins to respond.

"Yes…Yes, well, ladies and gentlemen, what we have here is…a great misunderstanding. This precious child is innocent of any and all charges that have been brought forth against her. She is guilty only of being a joyful child, singing to herself and, yes, even in public. Praises to God, the same God you good people profess to following, not enchantments, not curses. This is a simple case of misunderstanding."

The young advocate's voice was calm and peacefully pleading to the crowd for their support. As he turned to face the bishop, his expression and tone changed as well.

"A misunderstanding that saw this child abducted from her home and brought here to be tortured upon the behalf of her faceless accusers and forced into this erroneous admittance of guilt." Mr. Bodkins was just warming up as he glared back at the crowd and the bishop.

"Lilly has also been accused of walking in the woods alone. Dear people, she lives there with her mother, Lady Marguarette, in a charming little cabin—in the woods, as the good reverend tells me. Lilly's father died from yellow fever only two years ago, so you see, she must walk alone to and from school into and out from the woods every day. It is, quite simply, where she lives. Her mother cannot be expected to be with her at all times." Mr. Bodkins leaned down to Reverend O'Reilly for the details again before proceeding.

"And yes, she does pick herbs and flowers, for that is how they support themselves, by selling herbals to the people in the surrounding villages. She picks flowers for her mother because she wants her to remember the essence of life is a fragrant one of love."

He paused, looking around the room and into the eyes of the on-lookers with an ambivalent smile.

"So you see, ladies and gentlemen, Lilly Morgan is innocent, misunderstood, taken from her home without just cause. Let us be sympathetic—let us be just—and above all else, by God's grace, let us send her home. Thank you, ladies and gentlemen." Mr. Bodkins finished, and Reverend O'Reilly smiled, shaking his hand vigorously for a job well done.

The crowd erupted. People were hurling insults, yelling and screaming violent accusations at Mr. Bodkins and Lilly.

"She's put a hex on ya!"

"The little witch has confused your mind. She's got you under her spell, Mr. Bodkins!"

"Burn the witch with the others!"

"Set her troubled soul free from the devil. Burn her!" The crowd began to chant and stomp the floor. The reverend thought that the floor would collapse from their stomping.

"Burn her! Burn her! Burn the witch! Burn her! Burn 'em all!"

Mr. Bodkins looked at Reverend O'Reilly aghast at the outcry. Bishop Van Buren grinned, motioning for the court officers to remove Lilly and the others from the courtroom and transport them to the Place of Purification.

The Place of Purification was a mile outside of town upon a hill overlooking Salem. It was a prominent point where all could see the justice of the court carried out. Five new poles had been set up earlier in the morning in anticipation of the convictions.

Black charred bits of wood covered the slope where previous sentences had been served. Each thirteen-foot pole sat three feet in the ground with ten feet towering above the accused and the crowd of gawkers. Sticks specially dried for quick lighting were stacked around each pole, and the accused was tied by their hands, which were wrapped around the pole behind them. Their feet rested on a small platform and were lashed together and strapped to the pole as well.

Many alleged witches and wizards had been freed on this hill, where each woman and one scared girl stood strapped to their tree, awaiting the Flame of Freedom to arrive. The sanctimonious march of the Torch of Truth or Flame of Freedom, as some referred to it, made its way up the hill through the group of onlookers.

Wailing and tears filled the sky as rain began to sprinkle down again on Salem. Bishop Van Buren ordered oil to be poured at the base of every pole. "Rain will not stop today's justice."

One by one, the oil-soaked points of purification were lit. Black smoke filled the sky, and flames arose. Crying turned to wailing; wailing turned to screaming as pain and flames engulfed the accused one by one. Bishop Van Buren and the rest watched with a mixture of satisfaction, relief, and disgust.

Lilly cried and murmured a song through her tears that no one heard. The flames crept closer, blacker, hotter; higher and higher they came. Lilly sang until she could not stand the pain any longer. As the flames overtook her body in a violent rush, her soul screamed.

High-pitched screams pierced the night.

"Aah! Aaah!"

Grandma Bertie was startled awake and was sitting straight up, holding her breath. Then she heard the screams again. Jumping from her bed, she sprinted down the hallway to Margie's room, where she heard the bloodcurdling screams.

Molly rolled off the couch in the living room, where she was camped for the night because of Gus's snoring and Margie's crying, and stumbled her way to Gus's room. She opened his door, and the window immediately slammed shut. Molly shook Gus awake from his screaming. He sat up hugging his sister in a cold sweat, shaking frantically.

The crest of the morning sun turned the horizon pink just above the tree line along the hills of Willow Branch as two otherworldly jack-o'-lanterns weaved their way through a jungle of tall grass along a narrow dirt path. They carried a tub of prized dirt toward a shattered greenhouse that sat at the back of a fenced-in yard near the railroad tracks.

One lowered its gnarly hand into the bucket and tossed the soil onto the ground. They entered the dilapidated greenhouse, filled a long, narrow tray with the remaining soil from the bucket, and climbed onto the table and into the tray filled with fresh soil that sat in the center of their new home. As the sun rose higher in the morning sky, two hollow orange pumpkins sank their roots deeper into their place of refuge. They had not found what they had come for, but they found what they needed to survive in the world of the living—blood.

Red lights flashed atop several police cars scattered along a slip of road in front of Hillmart on Winding Hill Road. Police officers were combing the area for clues to an apparent theft and murder. A K9 officer followed his dog, but the trail ended within the perimeter of the parking lot.

Officer Sims and Chief Sergeant O'Reilly stood inside the convenience store that looked as though a tornado had hit it on the inside. Products were scattered everywhere, and shelves were overturned onto the victim. They were taking a statement from Noah Baker, a seventy-year-old part-time clerk who had found the victim and called the police.

"Tha's right. I came on at 5:30 a.m. an' saw that nice-lookin' black car parked with the driver's side door open, an' the engine was still runnin', an that radio was blarin' somethin' awful, so I turned it off, you know. An' I noticed the door to the store was open too, so I go to close it an'…"

Officer Sims finished his long pause, shaking his head, "And you entered the store and found the deceased. Correct?"

"Tha's right. An' I… Oh, I don' know 'is name. It's always someone new, you know. Yep, always someone new behin' that counter these days. They don' last too long. You know, either too lazy, thieves, or they can't handle the hours. Or the place gets robbed. An' they don' stay long after that, you know," Mr. Baker said with a perplexed look on his face. "An' the place gets robbed a lot, you know, bein' so close to the innerstate an' all."

"Mr. Baker, did you touch anything? Move the deceased or anything?" Sergeant O'Reilly asked.

"No! I didn' go near…when I saw… No," Mr. Baker said with a slight shiver. Chief O'Reilly answered the radio that was clipped to his shoulder harness. The message was brief, and he reclipped his radio.

"Thank you, Mr. Baker. Now if you'll go see Ms. Reynolds so that she may take your prints, then you may go home."

Turning to Officer Sims, he began to speak again. "A mailman says that an elderly lady by the name of Timmons did not greet him at the mailbox as she does every morning, so he decided to take it to her and saw the door open. He looked inside and found two mummified bodies on the floor. That's four bodies mummified like this one—in two days. They didn't produce them that fast in ancient Egypt. I believe that Willow Branch has a serial killer on the loose.

"Find out who belongs to the black Charger and meet me at this address. I'll be there checking out the scene there the rest of the morning." Sergeant O'Reilly tore a piece of paper from his notebook and handed it to Officer Sims, his partner in training.

He saw something green in the hand of the victim. Chief O'Reilly bent down for a closer look. He took his handkerchief from his pocket and lifted a leaf from the victim's hand. It was familiar to him, but it was out of place and out of season. It was a leaf from a pumpkin vine. He considered it as he held it in his hand, looking at the scene around him. He noticed strange swirling patterns of dirt and gravel dust in the front half of the store up to the victim but none beyond the body. He did not know what to make of it.

———————

Sergeant Patrick O'Reilly was a man with broad shoulders and thick black hair and who had grown up in Willow Branch. His family had been one of the founding families of the town. His father had been a minister at the Episcopalian church following in the footsteps of his great-great-grandfather. But Patrick had chosen law enforcement as his profession, and in the twenty-plus years on the force, he had never known of any murders happening in Willow Branch.

There had been missing children, like Billy Madison, thugs, like that of the logging industry, and always small-town hooligans or the occasional thief, but never a murder. This was exactly the reason why Patrick O'Reilly had chosen to come back to Willow Branch after college and train at the academy. Nothing out of the ordinary ever happened in Willow Branch.

As he stepped into Mrs. Timmons house, he knew that his sleepy little town had something very evil present within it. He knelt down next to the shriveled-up bodies and looked around. Royal casino playing cards littered the floor. He saw something else that made his insides twist: squiggly dirt patterns covered an otherwise spotless carpet and a greenish-white leaf similar to the one he had discovered at the Hillmart scene. Nothing else in the house was disturbed; the place looked like a museum. Everything had a place on a shelf or on the wall and not a speck of dust anywhere.

Sergeant O'Reilly recognized a photo of her and Paul Beal sitting on a cabinet in the living room next to the couch where the bodies were lying. They were always giving their support to the FOP fundraisers for the police department. They never missed a function where food and beverages were served. He knew they both liked to keep an open bottle close-by on all occasions, but that could not explain why they were the victims of such a heinous death.

Maybe it is time to consider retirement after all, maybe a beach house somewhere in Florida before the market takes a turn for the better, somewhere to lead a quiet, peaceful life before someone finds me dead, lying shriveled on the floor someday. A knock at the door startled him.

Officer Sims had arrived with some interesting news, and Sergeant O'Reilly, after regaining his composure, was glad for the distraction from his conflicted and morbid thoughts.

"Sir, I found the rental agreement in the glove box, and the Charger was rented by a Janice Johnson and get this—" He was cut off by Sergeant O'Reilly, whose eyes lit up.

"She lives next door."

"Yeah, how did you know?"

"Never mind that. Call, get a warrant, and let's pay Ms. Johnson a visit," Sergeant O'Reilly said.

"Already did on my way over here. It's on its way with a backup unit," Sims said with a smile. Sergeant O'Reilly gave him an approving nod.

"Then let's go take a peek!"

———

Grandma Bertie watched the children eating breakfast with great concern. They were poking at their cereal; no one was eating. Not even her famous waffles, pancakes, or eggs with bacon sounded good to them this morning. Three bowls of cold cornflakes sat in front of them; not even hot oatmeal with cinnamon and brown sugar could entice them this morning. Grandma Bertie was beside herself with worry.

Gus and Margie looked like zombies with eyes glazed over and distant stares. Neither one had said a word about why they were screaming, if it was a dream, or what they might have seen. They just sat staring at their cornflakes with no intent to eat them.

Molly was too busy observing them both to eat as well. She was certain Gus had another nightmare. *Gus could have been frightened by Margie's screams, but he sleeps like the dead, so that doesn't make sense. What's up with his window? That's at least the third time that it has slammed shut when I have opened his door. Maybe it's some weird air vacuum or, maybe it's just old.*

"Come, you two, we have to get going if we don't want to be late. And we *don't* want to be late!" Margie and Gus moved like the living dead, picked up their backpacks, and sloshed toward the door. Grandma Bertie and Molly shared a glance of concern. Molly kissed her grandmother good-bye and followed them out the door.

———————

Officers Sims and O'Reilly exited Mrs. Timmons's house through the front door and turned to the left through the yard toward the Johnson house that sat next door. Looking down, Sergeant O'Reilly noticed a trail of pale green leaves leading to a broken window at the Johnson home. They matched the ones that he had found in the living room where Mrs. Timmons and Mr. Beal lay nearly petrified. The front door stood open; they pulled their guns as they entered.

Inside was a disaster area, much like the scenes at Hillmart and the home of Carl Hughes, Margie's stepfather, but something felt different. To Officer O'Reilly, this felt like someone was looking for something or someone and was in a hurry. The Hughes home seemed more calculated and deliberate, reminding him of the time when his wife had left him fifteen years ago, destroying most of his earthly possessions before she went.

Emotion—emotion was the difference. But these two neighboring houses were the work of the same villain. He was certain of that; he found many more leaves inside the Johnson house that matched the previous crime scenes, but they found no bodies. Officer Sims watched the sergeant pick up another leaf from the floor.

"What's up with all of the leaves?" he asked.

Sergeant O'Reilly replied, "What do we know? We have four crime scenes, four mummified bodies at three of the crime scenes, pumpkin leaves at all four scenes, an abandoned car, two missing persons, one where two juveniles happened to report the first crime from the first scene no less—" Sergeant O'Reilly stopped in midthought.

"What is it?" the rookie asked. "Wait a minute. You don't think those kids or Mrs. Johnson could have possibly had anything to do with this, do you?"

"I can't imagine it, but we are going to find out. Go to the school and bring the Johnson children and meet me at the old farmstead at the corner of Jackson and Lantern."

"Okay, but how will—"

"You'll see my car!" Officer O'Reilly said, shaking his head. He watched his young partner leave in his squad car and wondered how quickly the department would crumble once he retired. *How will they get along without me? What do I care? I'll be on a beach workin' on a good sunburn.*

———

Grandma Bertie sat at the kitchen table; she had not moved since the children had left for school. She had been in deep thought, very concerned about the events of night. She snapped out of her daze, knowing that she had something very important that she needed to do this morning, but she could not remember what it was.

So she decided to clean. Cleaning anything always seemed to lift her spirits and clear her mind. Bertie decided to start with the kids' bedrooms. Her stiff legs did not seem as enthusiastic about moving this morning as they had during her run the day before. She got up from the table. She was still a bit sore from her latest training run. The Pittsburgh Marathon was coming up sooner than she cared for. Grandma Bertie did not feel ready for her first marathon race, but she felt almost certain that no one ever was.

Before taking another painful step, she lowered her head toward the floor. Stretching was new to her, but Grandma Bertie enjoyed the way it made her feel—young and free to change directions without fear. When her hands gradually touched the floor, she began to control her breath, allowing the muscles in her back and shoulders to catch up with the pliable muscles now in her legs. She had not always been able to accept change in her life; adapting to new ways of doing things was very difficult for her.

Steven had been unaware of his influence upon Bertie with his ability to respond gracefully to various difficult issues. She had observed him in action for two years while he cared for his dying wife. For two years, Bertie watched him tending to Glenda's needs, and never a harsh or exasperated word came from his mouth. Bertie was ready to do so for him on occasion when Glenda would say awful and mean things about him, but Steven would stop her short with a loving glance.

He explained to Bertie that it was not Glenda speaking harshly toward him but the pain, and he could accept that. He had taught her how to love another unconditionally. Bertie still found it hard to do; she even wondered if she was even capable of such love, but Steven and the children made a good practice field for her efforts.

Bertie curled her spine, starting at her hips, until her head sat on top of her shoulders again and twisted; after feeling a couple of pops along her spine, she was ready to clean. Bertie opened her cleaning closet, grabbed a very old broom with a twisted wooden handle and natural bristles. She decided that Gus's room needed it the worst, so she leaned into his bedroom door to push it open.

Clothes and a collection of LEGOs littered the floor, making it difficult to even get into the room. The toil of unconditional love hit Bertie in the face like a heavyweight champion. Gus had been in her house a sum total of ten hours; nine of which he had been asleep, and still somehow his room looked like a natural disaster area.

Grandma Bertie shook her head, smiled, took a deep breath, and put her broom in the corner while she began Operation Pick Up. But before she could see much progress, she heard a knock at the front door.

Well, I wonder who that could be. Steven said he'd be busy all day mowin' yards.

Grandma Bertie swung open the heavy oak door to find Officer Sims and Sergeant O'Reilly standing on her porch with Gus, Molly, and Margie between them.

"What in the world!" Grandma Bertie said, disbelieving her eyes.

"May we come in? We would like to ask you and the children some questions," Sergeant O'Reilly said.

"Sure. What's this about, Patrick?" she asked. Officer Sims glanced at the chief, surprised that she would address him so casually. Sergeant O'Reilly saw the look of concern on his face and decided to fill him in on a little personal history.

"James Johnson, Ms. Bertie's son, and I graduated high school and then basic at Camp Pendleton together."

"Oh! So you were friends," said Officer Sims.

"Not exactly," Grandma Bertie said. Officer Sims felt the chill from her tone and wondered what the full story was. "Come on in and have a seat in the front room. Would you care for some coffee or tea?"

"No, thank you. We won't be staying long."

Officer Sims dejectedly put down his arm and closed his mouth. Coffee sounded really good to him; he had missed his usual two cups on this busy morning.

"Ms. Bertie, this morning we found three more bodies in the same condition as Mr. Hughes." Margie's face went pale.

"Carl's dead?" Her voice quivered and she began to shake. The trauma of that moment had been blacked out from her memory. "Do we have to do this in front of the children?" Grandma Bertie asked as she put her arm around Margie.

"Yes, I am afraid so, ma'am," said Chief O'Reilly. "We have now four mummified bodies, an abandoned rental car belonging to Janice at the Hillmart by the interstate. We also found a body in a similar state as Mr. Hughes inside the store and two more at

Mrs. Timmons's house. The Johnson home had been broken into also. And the only lead and witnesses we have are your grandchildren and your missing daughter-in-law. There has been evidence connecting all four deaths." Sergeant O'Reilly looked at them all. There was a very long uncomfortable silence; Sergeant O'Reilly gazed at them as cold as stone. "When was the last time that any of you saw or spoke to Janice?"

"That's Mrs. Johnson," Bertie snapped. Sergeant O'Reilly felt the invisible jab to his heart; he had always been in competition with James, Bertie's son, in everything, even love. Bertie still held Sergeant O'Reilly responsible for allowing obvious evidence against the Cutter Logging Company to be thrown out of the court case involving Melinda, Margie's mother, because of a technicality with his evidence-collection methods. Without that evidence, the prosecution had no case. She suspected foul play on Patrick O'Reilly's part, but of course, no one could prove it.

"And we haven' seen or heard from her since she left last night around 8:45 p.m. This doesn' make any sense. Why would she rent a car when I told her that I would pay for her to fly?" Gus and Molly looked at her as if she had lost her mind.

"Grandma! Mom is missing!" they shouted. "And Mrs. Timmons is dead. Who would do such a thing?" Molly asked Sergeant O'Reilly.

"We were hoping you two had some answers for us."

"We told you everything we know already," Molly snapped. "Are you looking for our mother?"

"The only real lead we have is you two and your missing mother. We have four mummified bodies drained of all of their fluids, your mother's abandoned ride at one of the crime scenes, and...pumpkin leaves at every scene, including your house," Sergeant O'Reilly said.

"Now wait a cotton-pickin' minute! Are you sayin' Janice and the kids had somethin' to do with these deaths?" She glared at both officers. "That's your conclusion? Janice was on her way to

Minneapolis for a job interview, and now she's missin'! Yes, I should have told you about findin' Margie, but I forgot. It has been a hectic mornin'. I am sorry, but the kids have been with me since their mother left. They have alibis. Please do everything you can to find Janice," Grandma Bertie pleaded.

"They don't have a sound alibi until we find their mother. Until then, they are all suspects," Sergeant O'Reilly said.

Grandma Bertie heard car doors slam shut in her driveway. She glanced out the picture window and saw a blue car with Child Services painted on the side of the door. A handsome tall black man and a roly-poly middle-aged white woman were headed toward the front door.

"What's Child Services doin' here?" she asked with a sick feeling in her stomach.

"Ms. Bertie, now that Margie has been located and to this point has no known relatives, the state assumes responsibility until a suitable home may be found for her," Officer Sims explained.

"*Over my dead body!*" Grandma Bertie roared. "She is my god-daughter. I'm takin' care of her now."

"I am truly sorry, ma'am, but the state only recognizes family as blood relatives, not spiritual relatives. You can petition the state for custody, but I must warn you that at your age, you may not qualify as a fit for her guardian," Officer Sims said.

Grandma Bertie sat in a stupor; she had assumed that she would be Margie's caretaker if something ever happened to Margie's parents. Legal guardianship was not part of her vocabulary. The agents of the state stood knocking at the front door. Grandma Bertie rose from her seat and disappeared down the hallway toward her bedroom.

The knocking continued. It was an awkward moment; no one in the living room moved until Sergeant O'Reilly finally stood and opened the door. He began to explain the situation to them briefly as they entered.

A round middle-aged woman with short brown hair and rosy cheeks made her way toward the children. Molly hugged Margie like a suit of armor; Gus moved between Margie and the intruding agents. The round woman bent down with an elfish smile, looked Gus in the eyes, and then, looking past Gus, spoke to Margie.

"Hi, Margie, my name is Cindy Armstrong, and I am here to help you find a new home."

"I don't want a new home! I want to stay with Ms. Bertie. She is like a grandmother to me, and these two are like my brother and sister! Why would I want to find another home? This has always been more of a home to me than at Carl's house."

"I understand, sweetie. Ms. Bertie is a very nice woman but—" Bertie reentered the room. Ms. Armstrong began to address Grandma Bertie with her impish grin.

"Ms. Bertie, please understand that we wish that we could leave Margie with you. It is better for everyone involved. However, no legal will has been found, and no attorney has of yet come forth with the testament of the parents as to Margie's guardianship. We must assume that no document exists, which is unfortunately too often the case with younger couples. No one ever plans on dying so young, which leaves much responsibility to the state. I am sorry. If only you were a blood relative, Margie's grandmother, this would not be an issue."

"I am her grandmother," Grandma Bertie said, handing Ms. Armstrong a file folder. "This is her birth certificate and a certified letter with DNA results that attests to the fact that Margie is my son's daughter." The room was filled with silent shock. Bertie knelt down in front of the children. She looked each one in the eyes.

"I am sorry that you all found out this way, but it has been in everyone's interest to keep Melinda's secret. Margie, your mother told me when you were born that you were my grandchild, but she asked me to swear to her that no one would know. She did not want to hurt Janice. Your dad knew, but the military life kept him away, and he never saw you beyond the photos that your mother had sent him.

"She never stopped loving him. The last time that we all saw him… Well, there is a reason you and Gus are so close in age. Gus, Margie is your sister, born two days after you. I'll never let anyone separate you again as long as I live. That's my promise to the three of you."

They could not understand. It was like a weird dream to them all, but it was a satisfying dream to wake up to. They looked at one another in confusion and disbelief, then the haze began to lift, and the reality of the emotional moment took over.

They hugged together, squeezing one another tightly, and tears of relief, tears of joy, and tears of sorrow flowed. Words were not possible in that moment, and none were needed. Agent Armstrong looked at the others and motioned them toward the door.

"These papers are authentic. James Johnson is her father, which makes Ms. Bertie Margie's grandmother, and with that, our work here is complete." Sergeant O'Reilly followed Ms. Armstrong and the others to the door before he turned back to speak to Grandma Bertie.

"Ms. Bertie, we will be in touch. And please, if you hear from Janice, let me—let us know. We are doing everything in our power to find her, I assure you." He closed the door behind him. The weeping huddle was oblivious to their exit.

Neither Gus nor Molly nor Margie was exactly sure what just happened, but they all knew deep down in their souls that they felt a joy that they had never before known.

Molly was the first to wipe her eyes dry and stand up. She was thinking of her mother and the horrible information that Chief O'Reilly shared with them. *Four identical deaths and pale pumpkin leaves at each crime scene. Where was her mother? Why was she not among those found dead? According to the curse legend, she should have been. But if she has not been found dead, then she must be alive!*

"Grandma! The jack-o'-lantern has mother! We've got to find her before it's too late. He may yet—" Molly couldn't say what she was thinking, and she quickly put the thought out of her mind.

"I know, dear. The police don't know what they are lookin' for, but we do. We won't stop lookin' until we find her."

The four of them immediately set out to search for her in Willow Branch Woods. Side by side they scoured the woods. Bertie led them to a small abandoned farmhouse with a dilapidated fence bordering what once must have been a quaint place to live. Molly noticed that Grandma Bertie seemed both relieved that they had found nothing and confused about where to go next. Margie suggested the Shelter Tree.

The Shelter Tree had been Margie's safe haven, a place where she and her mother used to rest from the heat or the thunderstorms during their special long walks in the woods. Margie looked inside the hollow of the sycamore and chose to ignore the secret passageway to an underground cavern that she had fallen into several days earlier. She needed for some things to remain her own since she had precious little that truly was hers alone. The sense of comfort and control that she felt at the hideaway was enough for her.

They marched back to Bertie's house disenchanted and exhausted. They entered the backyard through the gate and saw Steven Grogan pulling his trailer into his barn across the street after a long day of mowing lawns in the neighborhood.

After cleaning up, Steven went over for dinner. It was a meal filled with conversation. He heard all about the happenings of the day, from the screaming wake-up call to the entire student body of the middle school thinking that Gus, Molly, and Margie had been ushered to jail.

The awful deaths to Mrs. Timmons and Mr. Beal shocked him, but the terrible news of Janice's disappearance shook Steven the most. Steven glanced at Bertie when he heard that she had finally told the kids that they were siblings. He could see the relief, the worry, the fear, and the joyful satisfaction that she felt having the children together with her—with them. Everyone was ready for bed following homemade chocolate chip cookies and milk with the hope of a better tomorrow.

Steven knocked on the front door as he did most mornings, but today there was no answer inviting him in to eat his breakfast before it got cold. He did hear the television blaring from the kitchen. He let himself in only to find Bertie fixated upon every word of the news. He made his way across the room and turned it off.

"What are ya doin'?" Grandma Bertie yelled.

"Bertie, you can't keep this up. It's not good for you or the children. The authorities are doing the best that they can. They searched twenty-four hours a day for a week just to appease you, but they have found nothing. I am not saying that you should give up hope. But for the children's sake, you must move on with your life." Steven knelt down in front of her; Bertie looked away from his gaze.

"Bertie, six days has become six weeks. What if six weeks becomes six months or six years or maybe, God forbid, that Janice is never found? You can't blame yourself. You must move forward. The kids will be out of school very soon. You can't do this to yourself any longer. It's not healthy. This isn't your fault. It *never* was." She looked back toward him. His gaze was steady and loving. Bertie threw her arms around his neck and began to sob.

"You are right. I know that. I just needed to hear it from some-one else to believe it, Steven. Thank you." Bertie kissed him on the forehead. Looking him in his eyes, she kissed his left cheek and then the right. Continuing her gaze into his eyes, she kissed him on the lips. It was a kiss with meaning, with heart.

"I knew I should've gotten rid of that TV a long time ago," Steven said only half joking.

"When you marry me, you can do whatever you want. But if ya do that, how will you watch yer favorite show?"

"I've seen enough *CSI* reruns to last me another lifetime. Besides, I am sure you will keep me plenty busy." He leaned down and gave her a passionate kiss in return.

"Wow," Bertie said, "you think you know me pretty well, don't ya?"

"I do."

"Well, now that you mentioned keepin' you busy, I do recall a list I had written out for ya." Bertie searched her catch-all drawer for a notepad with Steven Projects printed in bold Sharpie.

"Hey, what time is it? I've got a busy day ahead of me. I'd better get." Steven made his way for the door before Bertie could find her honey-do list.

"It'll be here when you get back!" she shouted jokingly as he backed out of her driveway. He smiled as he waved good-bye.

Molly sat in social studies class hunched over, staring at the graded test that Ms. Neur placed in front of her. She knew that the last few weeks since her mother's disappearance she had not been as focused on her studies, but it wasn't until now that Molly realized how far she had dropped.

The B written in red marker screamed *buffoon* and *blithering idiot* at her in her mind. *What have I done? This will probably be on my transcript forever now.* Molly had been a straight A/A+ student since she started school in kindergarten. She prided in her intellect. An A– was unacceptable; a B was unheard of.

Molly realized that she missed her mother more than she ever thought possible. They had argued the last time that Molly saw her mother over what she could not remember. But she wished that she could go back in time and undo the hurt that she felt that she caused her mother that night and tell her that she loved her. That was something that was difficult for her to say to anyone, even her mother. Molly hated that about herself; she wished that in those moments that she was more like Gus, who spoke his mind to anyone who would listen.

The bell rang and startled her from her thoughts. Molly folded her test and stuffed it into her backpack as she headed out the door to math class. She hoped that her math final would be acceptable, but she wasn't holding her breath. *Two more periods and it is summer break. I can't wait.* Molly couldn't believe such a thought could have ever crossed her mind as she slowly shuffled down the hall.

The students were ready to explode like a time bomb ticking down to zero. Teachers lined the halls to keep the energy release to a minimum until the final bell rang, and then it would be everyone for themselves. Mass chaos would reign, and an explosion of uncontrolled energy would fill the halls one last time to finish the school year.

Margie and Gus were in most of the same classes, and Gus couldn't help but notice how much more engaged Margie had been these final six weeks of school. She had always been a good student, but she never volunteered any information unless called upon by a teacher to share an answer. He couldn't believe that she had raised her hand to share a voluntary book report with the class on the last day of school.

Margie stood at the front of the class, showing them a book about Native American herbology. He couldn't understand the author's name when she read it. She genuinely looked happy and content in her own skin for the first time in her life, and Gus was happy for her. He was proud of her and happy that she was his sister.

Davon, known to all as the school bully, was roaming the halls when he saw Margie through the open door. A mischievous grin curled on his face as he sat his books by the side of the door, out of sight from the teacher who was positioned at the back of the class grading tests at the last minute.

Davon tore a sheet of paper out of his notebook and stuffed it in his mouth. He chewed the paper into a chalky soaked ball. Margie finished her presentation with a smile as the class applauded her efforts.

Three, two, one, Davon launched his spit wad. It exploded on her left shoulder, splattering her hair and face with white pulp. The bell rang, and Davon disappeared down the hall. Margie stood in shock and disgust. Gus was fuming as Mr. Jones hurriedly passed out the graded final exams before the class vanished from the room.

"Are you all right?" Gus asked, knowing the answer.

Margie clenched her teeth and said nothing as Gus helped wipe the moist bits of paper from her shirt. Her mind raced with thoughts of revenge as she continued to pull bits of white from her hair as Gus carried her backpack full of books to the final class of the year.

Bertie decided to go for a run soon after Steven left her house. She had much on her mind and needed to clear her head. Running, like cleaning, always made her feel better. The Pittsburgh Marathon was coming soon, and she wanted to be at her best when it did.

She headed up the hill on Jackson Street to get the climb out of the way when she was fresh. She took in the sweet aroma of wild honeysuckle that was climbing a fencerow along the road. Bertie passed a white van that was pulled over on the side of the road. A man with an orange vest and hard hat climbed down from the telephone pole. She waved to him as she passed, but the man did not return the gesture. Bertie began to sort through her mental desktop as she reached the peak of Jackson Street.

Much had changed in her life in such a short period. Bertie lost herself in her thoughts as she kept her nine-minute-mile race pace.

Since she had Steven plow her garden to prevent the curse of the jack-o'-lantern from recurring, Bertie found a new passion to keep her and Steven occupied and in shape.

Steven had suggested endurance racing to Bertie as a lark. But to his ever-increasing lung capacity and dismay, she found it to be great fun and great exercise. Bertie forced him to train with her. They would make their way around town after breakfast four days a week. She would set the pace on foot, and Steven would ride his bicycle beside her. His knees prevented him from running and racing as she did in the local town events, but they trained together and traveled together for the mini marathons, bike races, and walks/runs in the nearby towns.

She was preparing for her first full marathon; she wanted the challenge. She needed the challenge. Running provided the push she needed to be her best. "Be your best self," she always told Gus and Molly. "No matter what anyone else is doin' or not doin', be your best self." She had been living by that motto for a long time and was not willing to stop simply because she was no longer able to do what she really loved, and that was gardening.

Gardening had been a very important part of her life for many years, but she had been determined to find another passion to fill that void in her heart. Endurance racing filled a small portion of that void. And though she hated to admit it, she had already found a large piece to the puzzle of her heart.

Bertie had known Steven Grogan all his life. She had watched him mature into a strong spiritually sound man who took care of his dying wife for two difficult years by himself when the doctors could do nothing more for her cancer.

They had been neighbors and friends for a long time. Steven and his wife, Glenda, had invited Bertie over for dinner and to play cards soon after she had moved in across the street after her husband died. They grew close very quickly. Often they would play cards into the wee morning hours, talking and laughing. There was always laughter in their home, even in difficult times.

When Glenda became ill, Bertie would visit with her to give Steven a break. Glenda Grogan asked Bertie to read to her one day, and she agreed without hesitation. Glenda handed her a well-worn Bible. Bertie's heart skipped a beat.

She picked up the Bible a little nervous. She had been in many churches in her lifetime but was less familiar with the Bible. Her experience with the Good Book came mostly as a child when she had heard stories that had frightened her, stories of devils, giants, bloody wars, plagues, and the wrath of God.

Worse still were the people that she had known that professed the Bible's truth but were mean to her, her family, and her friends through the years. She vowed to never become like them, so Bertie struggled with Glenda's request to read. As she reached out to take the Bible from Glenda's shaking hands, she put aside her fears and gave into the plea of her dying friend.

She struggled with many of the names and places as she read to Glenda. Bertie was amazed at what she was learning from this book of books. She read to Glenda every day and discovered that the Good Book wasn't so scary after all. It was full of science, history, and inundated with man's follies, trials, failures, and triumphs, but more importantly, it was filled with love, mercy, and forgiveness. She would ask Steven questions at dinner, and he would answer her to the best of his ability and understanding.

Bertie's spirit wrestled with what she was hearing and reading about forgiveness. She found forgiveness hard to swallow. She simply had been hurt too deeply just to let it go so easily. Steven continued to encourage her and patiently explained in his calming voice God's purpose of love and redemption through Jesus's death and resurrection.

Seeing how gracefully and peacefully Steven and Glenda handled the realities of her death caused Bertie to ask the question everyone asks themselves at some point in life.

"Is God real, and does he care about me?"

She did not know the answer yet, but she did know that she wanted to feel the peace that Glenda had in the face of death and that she and Steven had shown in their lives together all of the years that Bertie had known them.

The pinnacle came when Glenda asked Bertie to do something for her after she was gone.

"Bertie, Steven is a very strong man both physically and spiritually, as you know, but what you don't know is that he is very tenderhearted also. I hear him cry some nights and cannot help feeling responsible for his suffering."

"Glenda, you cannot blame yourself for dying. It is not your fault."

"Please, Bert, let me finish this. It isn't easy for me to say, and it is very important to me. Scripture says that it is not good for man to be alone. Well, it is not good for woman to be alone either. He's a good man, Bertie."

Bertie's brow pinched together as she tried to follow what Glenda was attempting to tell her, and then her eyes were opened to what Glenda was getting at. She was suddenly very uncomfortable sitting in front of her friend.

"I have seen how you both get along. I have seen the look in your eyes when he enters the room. You will be good for each other."

There was a long silence as Glenda allowed Bertie's mind to wander.

"I want this, Bertie. I want this for him, for you both. Bertie, when I am gone and when the time is right, I want you to know that you have my blessing to marry Steven."

Bertie could say nothing; she was deep inside of herself in shock. She had never imagined marrying ever again and certainly had not considered Steven, her best friend's husband, as a candidate. Bertie thought the idea was ludicrous, but she could not argue with a dying woman's request. She could only hug her friend and cry with her.

After Glenda's death, Bertie stayed away from Steven. She felt awkward, and their interaction seemed oddly strained for two people that had spent so much time together.

Bertie was on a ladder picking apples one day from the top step that read Do Not Step and reached as high as she could for a beautifully red plump apple when the ladder tipped. She clung onto the branch that she was picking from, swinging in midair and hanging ten feet above the ground.

Steven was in the yard across the street and saw her ladder tilting. He ran across the street and was standing beneath her as she hung by the branch. He reached up as high as he could but still could not quite reach her. She began to slip before he could get to the ladder.

"I am here, Bertie. I've got ya. You can let go now." She let go. Steven caught her in his arms. Smiling, he lowered her to the ground. He was still smiling when she turned and smacked him in the chest, taking him by surprise.

"I don't want to need you, Steven!" Bertie exploded and burst into tears as she hugged him. Steven was in shock. He gradually put his arms around her shoulders and began rubbing her back to calm her.

He knew something had been strange between them, but he did not know what, if anything, he had done to cause Bertie to shun him. He decided that when she was ready to talk, then she would let him know. He was hoping that this was the icebreaker that he had been hoping for. When she had gained her composure, she looked up at him.

"You've lost weight!" Bertie said in an accusing voice.

"I am not a very good—well, in fact, I am a terrible cook. Cereal tastes bland. I burn just about everything, and what I don't burn isn't fit for hog slop," he said, grinning from ear to ear. "It's good to see you, Bertie, but next time, I'd prefer it if you kept your feet on the ground. I know you don't need me, Bertie, but I am always here in case you do."

"Are you hungry?"

"Starving!"

"Come with me."

She took his hand and led him to her kitchen, where they spent the rest of the day and evening talking, laughing, crying, and eating really good food.

They spent more and more time together working in Bertie's gardens and orchard. He was always there when she needed something fixed that she could not do herself, and she was there when he ruined supper. He was a man of many talents, but cooking an edible meal had escaped him so far.

They grew very close, so close in fact that rumors surfaced at the church that they were getting married. Bertie always shied away from such talk. She was not sure she could marry any man again even if he was everything she had ever hoped for in a mate, all except for his inability to cook. Of course, no one is perfect.

Steven Grogan was close enough. After ten years of knowing this man, Bertie finally was willing to ponder the possibility of life with a partner. And she was excited about that future.

Over the years, she had chosen poorly, the men that she had known were lazy, drunkards, or downright mean, and those were the men that she had chosen for her husband. None of them lived very long, and she always felt the need to have another one for protection and shelter. Unfortunately, it was often times them that she had needed shelter from. The men in her life had always come with at a high price.

So choosing to marry Steven had been a decision that had taken some time to work through her past fears. She realized that

Steven *was* a man in every sense of the word and that he was, in her mind, a gift from God—and Glenda. God had fulfilled the longing that she had felt in her heart, and Steven Grogan was God's angel in her life. He made her heart overflow with hope, joy, peace, and above all, love. Bertie was ready; she felt very comfortable and confident that soon she would be Mrs. Roberta M. Grogan.

Bertie was beginning to get her second wind and feeling very good mentally as her worries began to fade. Then she remembered her garden, the one that had spawned the curse that brought a monster to life. It was still out there, and her daughter-in-law was still missing. Her mind raced frantically to find a solution that could bring peace back to her family, one that would correct the mistakes of her past and bring Janice back safe and sound.

The garden was no longer the problem, but the soil still had the potential. The monster, they were sure, had Janice. Bertie felt responsible and felt the need to find them to save her daughter from a gruesome death. If only she could find them.

Bertie was cutting through the Prairie Run neighborhood when she stepped on an uneven slab of sidewalk. She felt her foot turn and her ankle touch the cement. She went down hard as if she had been shot. Tumbling to a stop in the middle of the asphalt road, Bertie instinctively grabbed her ankle and curled into the fetal position.

———

The two o'clock bell rang at Willow Branch Elementary. The halls immediately filled with students in a mad rush to the gymnasium for the final period of the school year, a traditional farewell yearbook signing while a local band of overweight middle-aged men covered *their* favorite bands from *their* youth. It was a raucous time had by all.

Many of the staff charged with the task of supervision began to dance to the oldies. Mr. Applewood and Ms. Miller were doing the twist. They were too busy to witness the couple making out in the far corner of the gymnasium or the group of sixth graders that grabbed Gus from behind and carried him to the boy's locker room.

Davon Griggs, the notorious sixth grade bully, punched Gus in the stomach, and those holding Gus dropped him to the floor.

"Remember us, you little maggot?" Davon menacingly asked. "Maybe this will clear your memory."

He pulled a chocolate milk carton from his dirty jean jacket, not the small square size from the cafeteria but a large rectangular carton from Hillmart. The boy's wailed in laughter as Davon slowly poured chocolate milk over Gus's head.

Margie saw the bullies grab Gus from across the gymnasium floor; she burst into the boy's locker room as the last drop of milk exited the carton.

"Clean him up or I'm telling Mr. Applewood!" Margie screamed.

She startled the entire room of boys, even Gus. Davon played along.

"All right, you heard her. Let's clean him up!" Davon said with a devilish grin on his face.

The others understood him and grabbed Gus by his shirt and pants and held him upside down. They marched toward one of the toilet stalls.

"No! Wait! Leave him alone!" Margie yelled.

"Make up your mind. Boys, I think we should help her clear her head too. Grab her!" Before she could get to the door, they had her upside down. They dunked Gus and Margie several times in the toilet water, and on the final dunk, they flushed for good measure.

When they had finished with their fun, they taped Gus and Margie's hands, feet, and mouth with duct tape. Gus and Margie lay upon each other soaked to the skin and unable to move.

"See you in a couple of years," Davon said as he closed the door behind him.

The final bell rang, and the chaos in the gymnasium spread throughout the halls and out the front doors of the school. Molly stared sadly at her locker one final time as she gently closed the door. With a big sigh, she began to look around for Margie and Gus, who were supposed to meet her for their daily walk to Grandma Bertie's.

The hall became empty and quiet. Molly grew very concerned. She found Mr. Applewood and Ms. Miller in the corner of the gymnasium standing peculiarly close to each other. She cleared her throat to make her presence known. They turned around, startled to see her.

"Sorry to bother you, but I can't find my brother or sister anywhere," Molly said, a little embarrassed for everyone.

"Yes, well, Ms. Miller, if you will check the girls' locker room, I will begin our search in the boys' locker room." Mr. Applewood's suggestion to Ms. Miller had more than one purpose. Her hair, which usually was tied in a tight bun, looked like squirrels had nested in it.

The red-faced Mr. Applewood found Gus and Margie back-to-back, struggling to stand up. He took out his pocketknife and cut their bonds and let them tear the tape from their mouths.

"Who did this to you?" Mr. Applewood demanded. Gus was ready to spill his guts when he saw Margie glaring at him as if to say "Don't you dare!" They both stared at him in silence. "Very well, get outta here… And have a fun summer." Margie and Gus ran for the door. Gus turned at the last second.

"You too, sir, and you have something on your…" Gus motioned at his face in a circular motion with his finger and left in a flash. Mr. Applewood turned curiously toward the mirror that stretched the length of the room; to his horror, he had bright red lipstick covering his face.

On the way to Grandma Bertie's house, Gus explained to Molly what had happened. Margie was visibly enraged and walked a few steps ahead of them. She was already planning her revenge.

———————

Bertie was clutching her sore ankle and did not notice the truck pulling a trailer full of mowing equipment stop behind her. It was Steven; he had just finished another yard and was headed to the next when he saw someone in the road.

"Bertie? Are you all right? What happened? " he asked, placing his hand under her shoulders.

"Twisted my ankle." She grimaced. Steven slid his right arm under her knees and lifted her to his truck.

"I'll take you to the hospital for X-rays."

"No, you won't!" she hollered. "Take me home. I'll be all right. I just need to get off my feet and ice it. I could use some Arnica Montana in gel and tablet form from Nature's Pharmacy in town, if you don't mind though."

"Bertie, are you sure? What if it's broken?"

"It's not. I can tell it is just badly sprained. Ice, arnica, elevation, and gentle motion will get me back quicker than a cast or boot that the doctor will surely put me in." Steven shook his head but did not argue with her. He took her home and placed her on her couch with pillows, propping up her ankle.

"Okay, need anything else before I go?"

"Nope, just the arnica."

"I'll be right back." Steven bent down and kissed her on the cheek. He returned fifteen minutes later with her order and her favorite fountain drink from Hillmart convenience store. He also had bought a cryowrap, a cooler that, once filled with ice and water, had tubes running iced water into a brace that wrapped around her foot and ankle. It was reported to help decrease swelling fifty times faster than ice alone. He plugged it in, and it hissed as it began to pump cold water through the tubes to the injured ankle.

Steven coated her foot and lower leg with arnica gel. Bertie placed three tiny arnica tablets under her tongue for good measure. Arnica Montana was a flowering herb once used by Indians for many maladies, but her version was a powdered homeopathic tablet for pain and edema according to the label on the bottle.

"What's edema?" Steven asked Bertie.

"It's a fancy name for swellin'," she said, wincing as she adjusted to the cold of the cryowrap.

She felt confident that her recovery would not be as long as the average sprain, but she also knew that her first marathon would not be in Pittsburgh, not this year anyway. Steven was willing to stay with her all day to care for her, but she knew he had a busy schedule. Bertie encouraged him to leave and said that she would be fine but that she would need him to help her with feeding the kids supper.

"Okay, I'll fix chicken noodle sou—on second thought, I'll bring us Chinese for dinner tonight instead," he said smiling.

"Sounds good," Bertie said with a sigh and a relieved grin. She laid her head back, and Steven covered her in a blanket.

"You rest, and I'll see you this evening." He kissed her and was gone.

Steven was in deep thought about Bertie's injury when he glanced to his right to notice a lawn with five-foot-tall grass growing out of control in one of the last remaining bank-owned properties that he had yet to get to during this busy spring. He sighed as he passed the property, knowing that one day he would return to attack that lawn.

Beyond that forest wall of grass at the end of a narrow dirt path stood a greenhouse with shattered glass panels. Inside was a long table. On that table, two pumpkins, after days of withering, finally collapsed upon themselves with rot.

Two fearful spirits finally returned to the pit; they had taken their time returning. Neither one wanted to deliver the news of their very brief visit to the world of the living. They crept into their master's chamber. Satan sat upon his throne of human bone; he snarled at them as they approached.

"Your lordship, we did what you instructed us to do. We... but... Something happened," one said, looking at the other for confirmation, who nodded in return. "And our vessels... Well, they dried up and rotted away."

"Did they?" the devil asked in a low disbelieving tone. "Humor me please. What exactly did you do?"

"Well, we came up through the porthole, and it was just as he had said, but when we arrived at the woman's house, no one was there. We were desperate for strength, so we went next door and found a convenient replacement sacrifice. Then—"

"Yes, I know. Spare me the rest of your pitifully stupid tale. Your victims arrived shortly after your encounter with them, and I heard all about it. You chose an eighty-five-year-old man with emphysema and an arthritic ninety-year-old woman as a substitute, and you wonder why your shelf life was so short." The devil scowled. "They had no more shelf life! Then you trailed after her and found an empty car, but to your delight, the clerk was still behind the counter. So you helped yourself to a midnight snack on a pothead and junk-food junkie? There was no power left in their blood! You fools! Get out of my sight before I throw you into the pit myself.

"Now I must wait for more vessels to grow before unleashing my revenge upon the earth. This time I will send a multitude. With a pumpkin army, I will do my biding with swift, merciless vengeance." The devil howled with delight at the thought.

The devil summoned the Mara with a wave of his hand. A green mist hovered across the floor of sulfur and ash until her form came to a rest before the Prince of Darkness.

"I want you to monitor the boy and the girl again. We will use their strange connection with the jack-o'-lantern to discover his plans. Jack should have never made another deal with me. I will make certain that I come out the victor this time. Then I will throw his worthless body and soul into the pit. Vengeance will finally be mine!" The Mara vanished into the darkness.

———————

The short summer break flew by in a routine of business for everyone. Steven had been a good nurse and finally insisted that she get an X-ray taken, and of course, Bertie *had* chipped a bone in her ankle. She wore a boot for six weeks, and by the July 4 weekend, she had started physical therapy.

Steven had played nurse to Bertie when he wasn't keeping up with the fertile lawns of the neighborhood. The summer's brief drought did, however, slow down the growth enough to allow him to catch up with most of the bank's foreclosure properties.

Molly planted flower beds and then painted them while Gus was busy himself with playing baseball. His team, the Blue Sox, was terrible, the worst in the league, but Gus was still voted most valuable player in the league. And for one week, they played flawlessly and won the season-ending tournament. Gus was thrilled with the win but was happier that the season was finally over so that he could have some free time before school started.

Gus's free time was short-lived as Steven recruited him to help with mowing the neighborhood lawns. Gus hated to work. He was more than ready for the cool weather of fall so that the grass would stop growing and football, which was his favorite sport, would be in full swing, but fall seemed too far away for him. He hated working so much that he secretly hoped that school would start again soon. Gus felt that he might be losing his mind for even thinking such a thought.

Gus and Molly kept themselves busy so that their minds would not dare to wonder about their mother. The thought of never seeing her again was too painful to dwell on. The police had run out of leads, and Sergeant O'Reilly still was not convinced that the two of them did not know more than they had told him.

Margie continued her herbology lessons with Grandma Bertie every morning and was learning at a rapid pace. She had taken long walks in the woods most days, and when she was not walking by herself, she was locked in her room reading—studying.

She knew the story of the witch from the witch's journal. The Lady Marguarette was a simple Irish woman abused by her loathsome husband, but her life was ordinary until she received the *Book of Spells* from a hooded man that appeared and vanished mysteriously.

It was this book of spells that she could not stop reading. Margie was obsessed with it like a chocolate craving. She had to have more. After copying a page or two, she would round up all of the ingredients and practice the spells at the Shelter Tree, far away from prying eyes. Margie was intensely focused on her goal, her skills were sharp, but bringing the dead back to life required more than skill—it required that someone must die.

The summer was coming to an end, and Janice Johnson was still missing, and the murders of four citizens of Willow Branch still went unsolved. School would be starting up again soon, and Grandma Bertie was beginning to run again for the first time in months.

"Bertie, are you coming?" Steven asked, holding out his glove-sized hand for her. She snapped out of her thoughts and grabbed his hand with a big smile on her face, and as she bounced up out of her seat, she kissed him on the cheek.

"What's that about?" he asked, smiling back at her with a twinkle in his eyes.

"You make me happy, that's all."

"Well, you would make me very happy too if you would bring yourself outside so that we can get this run in before it decides to rain again," he said, still smiling.

"Oh, right. I had nearly forgotten."

"Don't tell me now that you have agreed to marry me after all of these years that your mind is starting to go," Steven said, smiling even wider.

"Oh you, get outside before I give you a piece of my mind!" Bertie bellowed, pushing him out the door for their morning run.

Margie was alone again at the Shelter Tree. She needed the time and space to master her favorite spell in the *Book of Spells* so that she could become proficient enough to make it work, at least make this one work, the one that would reunite her with her mother again.

She would read a spell twice and then copy it onto a legal pad of white ruled paper with a pink or purple ink pen, whichever she found first at the bottom of her backpack that day. This method helped her to memorize and learn each spell. Day after day at the Shelter Tree and many nights locked in her room, Margie would study, write, and contemplate the true purpose of each spell and incantation. Many were merely medicinal, some were for protection from illness, and others were more confusing, darker in purpose.

Transfiguration was a section in the big book that seemed to turn one thing into something else. Margie read this section carefully. She found the scribbled side notes difficult to make out but thought one would turn a potato into steak and another a turnip into a pumpkin. *Next time Grandma Bertie fixes ham and beans, I will be tempted to go to my room and see if I can't make a pizza,* Margie thought.

By the end of August, she had copied the entire *Book of Spells* and had what she thought was a good working knowledge of each spell. One spell in particular she studied more than any other and read it every night before bed. Margie would then dream of running through the woods with her mother until Grandma Bertie would knock on her door every morning with her wake-up call.

"Breakfast, dear."

Margie finally felt ready and courageous enough to attempt the spell. She was ready to meet the author of the note that she had found in her backpack months ago. She was so ready to see her mother again that she was willing to do whatever it would take to bring her back.

The monotony of her writing allowed her mind to wander and wonder. She thought back to Carl, gritting her teeth. His last phone conversation that she had overheard she was certain was between Carl and someone at the Cutter Logging Company.

She was so certain that she told her attorney during an appointment concerning her lawsuit against the logging company. Officer O'Reilly promised to look into the matter; her attorney also promised Margie that he would look into the phone records. Officer O'Reilly didn't seem to appreciate her attorney's desire to help.

Is he an egomaniac, or is there something else going on? She thought. *It has been months since the murders. Gus and Molly's mom is still missing, and he has yet to find any suspects besides them. That seems weird to me. I'd better get back to the house before Grandma Bertie comes looking for me.*

Margie packed her backpack full with her scribbles and headed out from the base of the sycamore. She glanced around to see if anyone was near before she covered the secret trapdoor to the underground cavern. She had not been down there since she furnished the door where a false floor had been keeping it hidden for years, but Margie wanted to make sure that no one else could find it. Dirt and leaves flew left and right as she hid the secret door. When she was satisfied, she headed down the hill toward Grandma Bertie's.

"Well, that's disturbing," said a man with a deep voice that had the chest rattle of an experienced smoker on the other end of the line. "She may be more of a problem for us than Carl ever was. You know what to do."

"Look, I have covered for your flunkies, given you vital information on this case and others like it over the years, misdirected evidence, and even falsified evidence to keep you in the clear many times, but I am not about to kill anyone, least of all a little girl. Do I make myself clear?"

"Are you gaining a conscience after all this time?" The man that spoke from the other end of the line chuckled. "Let me make myself clear. You *will* do this, and you will retire a very rich man on the beach of your choice. Refuse me and... Well, let us just say that retirement age won't be an option for you."

"Are you threatening me? I'm still the—" The hum of a dial tone filled his ear. He looked at the receiver in anguish as he hung up the phone. Immediately, the phone rang again. He took a deep breath before he picked up the receiver.

"Yes?"

"We'll take care of the kid. Call it a tradition, a family thing. And you keep the heat off us. Right? This will be all behind us as soon as there are no more plaintiffs to press us. No witness, then there is no case. Am I right? And you, my friend, *will* retire to some sunny place with a nice bankroll so that you can live like a king for the rest of your miserable life. Right? Right." The hum of the dial tone rang in his ear once again.

────────

It was late; Grandma Bertie and Steven sat at the kitchen table, listening to the eleven o'clock newscast while Steven was humbling Bertie in another hand of rummy. Her grandchildren were asleep; they had had a very busy day, swimming at the community pool.

Officer Sims slouched in his squad car parked on the side of the road at the top of Jackson Street overlooking Bertie's farmhouse. Sergeant O'Reilly had rotated him to the night shift so that he could keep a close watch on the only suspects that the department had in the quadruple murder case.

Watching Steven Grogan cross the street numerous times was the highlighted event. For three nights straight in July, all three of Bertie's grandchildren stormed the front yard, chasing lightning bugs. It had been a long dreadfully hot, uneventful summer. Officer Sims leaned back upon the headrest and closed his eyes to rest for a moment; soon he was snoring louder than Gus.

Molly appeared from the bedroom. Dragging her blanket behind her, she had her pillow under her arm. The card players watched her shuffle around the corner as she headed back to the couch in the front room. Bertie watched her snuggle in.

She leaned her head toward Steven and whispered, "Poor dear. Gus must be snorin' again."

Steven whispered back, "Rummy."

"Again? Oh, Shaw!" Bertie sighed. Steven scooted his chair back from the table and stood up. "Where you goin'?"

"It's late, Bertie, and I'm tired...of beating you...for one night anyway."

"You can't leave yet. I need another chance," she pleaded.

"Everybody deserves a second chance, Bertie. God made sure of that. That's also why he made tomorrow nights." Steven smiled, bent down, and kissed her on the check, the only side that she offered as she turned her eyes away from him.

"Fine. Have it your way tonight because tomorrow it'll be a different story." She glared, looking back at him with her arms crossed.

"As you wish, my love," he said, stepping out the front door on his way across the street. Bertie walked to the door, watched him enter his house, and closed her door for the night. Soon Bertie was in her bed, snoring worse than Gus and Officer Sims combined.

A white cargo van silently rolled with its headlights off next to Officer Sims's parked car. Four goons from the Cutter Logging Company looked at the sleeping policeman.

"Willow Branch's finest at work, boys," the driver said. The others snickered. "I'll pull up closer and let you out. Be quick and quiet. Remember, we need to make this look like an accident." The van coasted undetected down the hill on Jackson Street. It stopped at the bottom where Jackson intersects Lantern and let three burly men out with murder on their minds.

Margie woke up with the snoring of Grandma Bertie ringing in her ear, but she was thankful because she had fallen asleep against her will. Tonight she had planned to go below the Shelter Tree, hoping to meet the author of the note that she had found in her backpack months ago. She considered herself crazy for thinking anyone would actually be there, but Margie felt certain of it anyway. She slid out her of bed fully clothed; lifting her partially opened sash wider, she climbed through her bedroom window.

Three shocked men froze in the shadows at the rear corner of the house, watching in disbelief as their prey appeared through a window and scampered off into the darkness.

"Come on! We don't want to lose her."

They sped off after her, trying to keep pace. Chester, the fastest of the three, took off like he was shot from a cannon. The former Willow Branch High football star and school flunk-out flew through Bertie's backyard until he hit a fence post that struck him in the chest, knocking him flatter than any defensive lineman ever had. The four-inch black square post was the last remaining from Bertie's fencerow. Steven had left it to be extracted another day. When Danny and Bubba caught up to him, he was on all fours, gasping for air.

"Come on! Get up, or we're gonna lose her in those trees," Bubba said with hushed urgency into Chester's ear.

When she had cleared Bertie's backyard and made it into the woods, Margie turned on her flashlight and began to jog up the hill through the trees.

"She is making this a lot easier with that light," Danny said.

"Are you complainin'?" Bubba growled.

"No, I—"

"Shut up and keep movin' then!" Bubba said as he pushed Danny forward. Chester was slouched forward, still holding his chest, gasping for air.

Unaware of their presence, Margie made her way to the Shelter Tree. Even in the darkness, the Shelter Tree was a welcome sight for Margie. As she drew closer, she stopped a few yards short of the tree, frozen with sudden fright. She saw a glow coming up from the base of the hollowed-out tree. Her self-made trapdoor stood open. Her killers were closing in fast undetected behind.

Motivated by the anticipation of her mother's return prompted Margie to push back her fear and press onward toward her goal. She cautiously approached. The author of the note knew what she wanted and promised to help. Margie knew that she needed all the help she could get, and anyone willing to help her bring her mother back, she felt, was a true friend.

She made her way down the dirt ramp at the base of the tree. Margie cautiously crept down, wondering who her mystery friend was. Three murderous men were slowly approaching the tree.

Margie slid down the ramp under the Shelter Tree on her hands and feet, crab style. She knew this would keep the dirt off her clothes. Margie wanted no evidence to make Grandma Bertie suspicious about her dirty laundry. This was Margie's big secret, and until her mother was with her again, no one could know where she had been or what she was planning.

She hit the bottom with a thud and reached up carefully with her hand to be sure that she did not hit the low-clearing root that had knocked her out cold on her previous visit. The cavern was lit up by large hanging cages of light. She assumed that they were oil lamps or had large candles in them; she could not tell for sure. She still had no idea who had started them; the cavern seemed empty of life. She walked around to get a better look at the layout when she heard voices from above coming down the ramp.

Margie hid behind a collection of tall baskets at one end of the room. Three gruff-looking large men appeared to be looking for something. *Or someone*, Margie thought.

"Quiet," said the man with a scar on his face that ran from his ear to his mouth. "I know she's down here."

Margie's heart leaped in her chest, and a lump filled her throat.

"Find her!" he whispered. They fanned out in different directions, looking under the large round table that sat in the middle of the room. One tossed a stack of baskets into the air. Then a mysterious wind came out of nowhere and blew out the lights. Complete darkness filled the cavern.

"Hey!"

"What the—"

"Let go of me! Aah! Aa—" Danny's scream was silenced.

Chester and Bubba stood like statues in the dark, frozen in place with fear. They strained to see through the darkness and held their breath to hear any movement that would alert them to what was happening. Chester couldn't stand the silence.

"What's goin' on? Danny? Danny? Where are yo—aah, aah! Aa—" Silence again permeated the dirt hall.

Bubba's shaking hand fished out a metallic lighter from his jean pocket. Its flame flickered in the darkness, giving him little light and less comfort than he had hoped. "Guys! This ain't funny, man! Chester! Danny? I mean it! Where are you?"

"I'm right behind you," a deep rasping voice said from above and close behind Bubba, who was quivering in his own skin.

He turned to see a green translucent orb glowing in the dark. It seemed to float bodiless before him. Triangular flame-filled eyes appeared, and then Bubba could see a jagged-toothed grin light up as the face of a jack-o'-lantern was looking down upon him. Jack then opened his mouth wide.

"Aah! Aah!" Flames engulfed the poor wretched thug where he stood. As he crumpled to the floor, his wailing ceased. Margie watched in horror. With a tilt of his head, Jack filled the air with fire, and the oil lamps came to light again. And he spoke to the girl that was crouched petrified and hiding behind a pile of baskets.

"Margie, you need not fear me. I am here to help you. I am your friend Jack." The jack-o'-lantern said, staring at the baskets where Margie still hid. "Margie, these men were sent to kill you. They were employed by the Cutter Logging Company, who seems to want you dead very badly."

"How do you know that?" Margie asked, unable to contain herself as she stood to face the creature. "What are you?" She looked upon him in amazement, thrill, and dread.

"There is power in the blood of man, great, wonder-working power. I relieved them of theirs as I did with Carl, and I have learned much from them. Carl, your stepfather—"

"He was no father to me!" Margie screamed. "He was my mother's lousy husband!" The jack-o'-lantern observed her spirit and youthful exuberance with great curiosity and admiration.

"Carl loved your mother so much that when she died he could not bear to look at you because you reminded him of her. He did not hate you. He loved your mother and could not cope with life without her. You were an unfortunate casualty to his inability to move forward with his life," Jack said.

"You saved me from death, and now I have saved your life twice. I believe that means that you owe me a favor." The jack-o'-lantern stood before her, waiting for a response. Flames flickered inside his white hollowed-out gourd of a skull. Not even Bertie's special soil could completely restore him to health; two years without proper food and water had nearly ended the life in the little plant that Margie had rescued. She unwittingly revived the curse of the jack-o'-lantern in the process. His pale skull was a reminder of how fragile his existence really was.

Margie moved to her left, still facing the creature. She was determined to make the ramp until she bumped into the round table.

"Don't be afraid, my precious child. I will not hurt you," Jack rasped.

"You killed Carl and these men?"

"A necessity, I'm afraid," he said, and then his voice became cold. "Believe me, they would have done worse to you."

"How do you know that? How did you know I was coming here tonight? How did you know about this place?" she asked as her heart began to slow its trepid pace. Margie began to feel herself becoming calmer in his presence. She began to feel normal again, which surprised and confused her. *How can I trust this murdering creature? But I do.*

"This had been an old mine shaft before the witch bought it, then she transformed me into this," Jack said, showcasing himself before her. "Many years ago, this place was used to hide many things—slaves from the Confederacy, the witch's practices from the town, and, of course, me from the rest of the world.

"Marguarette was prompted by the devil in disguise, given a book of magic. She was taught by fellow women of the craft, and then, in a moment of rage and pity, she mercifully transformed me into this to hide me from the devil, whom I had deceived.

"I became her slave, one that needed hiding. She would have me enforce her revenge upon the towns that had her only child sent to be murdered for witchcraft. Lady Marguarette, the real Witch of Willow Branch, could not forgive herself or the townspeople.

"I did as she commanded, and then she tried to finish me!" the jack-o'-lantern bellowed. Flames shot from his mouth toward the ceiling. Margie did not flinch.

"I read all about that. What you say is true. I have read the witch's journal. She regretted ever transforming you, but even though you had treated her so poorly, she still felt obligated to help you. It wasn't until she lost her daughter that she snapped. When she finally came back to her senses, she knew you had to be stopped, that Satan had to be stopped. You are a tortured soul, Jack. I think I can understand how you feel a little bit." Jack looked at Margie in disbelief. "How did you know I was coming here tonight?" Margie asked still curious.

"Your blood is full of information, my dear. When you were helping me, I pricked your finger. I know your thoughts, past and present. We have a connection through your blood. You reminded Carl of your mother, and you remind me of my wife. The resemblance is curious to me."

"What do you want me to do for you?" Margie asked. Jack grinned.

"I want to live again! I want you to undo the witch's curse and transform me back into Jack Smythe. I am sickened by my existence. I don't want to hurt anyone anymore. I want to be human again! If you can do this for me, then you can bring your mother back also." Jack's eyes flickered full of hope. "I'll be your first test subject."

"Okay, I am ready, but I want you to do one thing for me before I transform you back." The flame in Jack's skull died just a little. He knew that he was still a slave to the young witch's whimsy.

"What would you have me do?"

"I want you to find the man responsible for my mother's death at the Cutter Logging Company."

"You would have me murder for you?" The jack-o'-lantern's eyes flickered with flame.

"Yes," Margie replied as cold as stone. "We need a sacrifice anyway, right? A trade-off for your transformation back to the living?"

Jack considered her resolve.

"I overheard a phone conversation of Carl's, and I know he was talking to someone high up at the Cutter Logging Company who had Mom killed. Lawyers are all vampires, sucking money and justice from the judicial system. They will never bring the case to its righteous ending. I want you to bring them to justice for me. I want them to pay for what they have done!" Margie yelled. Her eyes were full of fury.

Fire flickered in the skull of the jack-o'-lantern as jack considered Margie and his options.

"As you wish. I will do this for you, but it will not and cannot justify my transformation. Only righteous blood can do that. It seems that Carl has once again provided you with precious information by his blood. I know who is responsible. Meet me here next Saturday. You will be reunited with your mother very soon.

"Now I need to ask you another favor as you go," The jack-o'-lantern said as he turned his head and lit up another group of baskets stacked at the far corner. Behind them, Margie could see a figure lying on a blanket on top of loose straw.

Margie's face revealed what she was feeling inside: pure shock. Gus and Molly's mother, Janice Johnson, who had been missing for months, was still alive and lying in front of Margie.

"She is safe. The threat is gone for now." The jack-o'-lantern saw the look on Margie's face. "You are wondering why I haven't killed her like all of the others. I told you, I do not want to hurt anyone anymore. Her life was in danger, and I got to her before the others.

"Now take her. She needs nourishment." The creature grabbed the blanket that Janice Johnson was lying upon and dragged her behind him. "Follow me." Margie followed him toward a dark corner of the large room near the bottom of the ramp to the surface. The jack-o'-lantern blew flames from its jagged mouth, igniting torches that were staggered along the walls of a long corridor.

"This tunnel will save you some time," the jack-o'-lantern said. "Push, open the door when you come to its end, and it will lead you home. Now go before you are missed."

He handed Margie the blanket with Janice still sleeping drugged with a serum from the black needles that covered his limbs of vine. The serum had kept her asleep and alive in a near-vegetative slumber for months.

Margie struggled her way through the long corridor. The weight of Gus and Molly's mother was too much for her to handle at first, but she finally got into a rhythm and kept moving forward, stopping only when she hit a thick sheet of hanging spiders' webs.

Janice's head hit the dirt floor with a thud as Margie swiped at the clinging webs furiously. She waited very still for a couple of seconds, trying to determine whether she had any spiders crawling in her hair. She felt no movement, so she reached up as high as she could on her tiptoes and lifted the last of the lit torches out of its holder.

Margie used it to clear the remaining corridor of webs, lighting the torches as she came to them. When she had reached the end, she saw hinges on the left side of what looked like a wooden-slatted wall. She slowly turned to look back down the lit up corridor and wondered why and how this passage came to exist. She ran back to where Janice still lay, squatted down, grabbed the corners of the blanket, and leaned her shoulders forward to gain momentum again. She finally came to the end again with Janice in tow.

A green mist slithered its way through the maple tree outside of Gus's bedroom window. The branches began to coil into knots as the Mara moved toward the screen of Gus's opened window. She stood before him as a radiant beauty with long blond hair that shimmered in the moonlight and covered her bare back to her midthigh.

She placed one hand at the foot of his bed, preparing to climb on top of him and force the air from his lungs, when something in the corner of his room grabbed her attention.

Under a baseball jersey and cap stood a very old broom with natural coarse bristles bound to the stick by leather strings. Mara gnashed her teeth as she made her way toward the broom, watching Gus snore peacefully on his bed.

She was unnaturally drawn to the broom; the night hag struggled to break its spell over her but was unable to do so. She sat in the corner, watching Gus with her legs wrapped around the broom handle, and she began to count each bristle one by one.

Her beauty had been stripped away, and her true self shone in the corner illuminated by Gus's night-light. A very small childlike witch sat counting the bristles of the broom; her long hair and beautiful complexion had disappeared, revealing white strings of hair that barely covered her scalp, and white flakes covered her splotchy red skin. Razor-sharp teeth gnashed as she continued counting bristles.

Night hags were known in the old world countries for being notoriously poor with sums. Her dull mind and sharp nails made losing count commonplace. Brooms were often left in a bedroom corner to prevent bad dreams, for nightmares would only happen if the hag completed her count before the sunrise. Boo hags, as they were also known, had to move in darkness or risk being destroyed by the sun.

This increased the pressure that Mara felt as she tried to focus on each bristle. The longer she struggled, the more agitated she became for she knew that death came with the rising of the morning sun.

Gus yawned and sat up in bed before he reached for a glass of water sitting on his bedside table. Three or four gulps later, he replaced the glass on the table and scooted back under his sheets as he snuggled back into bed.

Gus opened his eyes and saw something out of the corner of his right eye. He sat straight up. His throat was parched again. His eyes were as large as dinner plates; his back was pressed firmly up against his headboard as he stared at the thing in the corner of his room hugging Grandma Bertie's broom. He struggled to scream, but his dry throat prevented him.

It looked at him with tiny red eyes and hissed. Gus found his voice. "Grandma... Grandma. Grandma!"

Grandma Bertie fell out of bed delirious, not sure what just happened. Then she heard Gus's screams again.

"Grandma!"

She ran into the hallway. Upon coming to Margie's door, she tried to open it, but the handle would not turn; it was locked.

"Grandma!"

Bertie raced two doors down and threw the door open. Molly was right behind her. They both froze at the doorway, staring in disbelief.

"Impossible," Molly mouthed. Mara turned toward the door, suddenly aware that she had been seen.

"You!" Mara snarled. Grandma Bertie charged, grabbing the broom. She swatted the night hag. Mara's screech deafened them momentarily as she fled through Gus's window and into the night. *Bang!* The window slammed shut behind her.

"No way!" Molly yelled.

"Grandma, what was that thing?" Gus squealed. Bertie was leaning against the wall for support, exhausted from the moment.

"That...thing was the night hag!" Molly chirped. "I read about it in a library book that I checked out earlier in the school year. She actually exists!"

"Well, you don't have to be so happy about it! What's a night hag anyway? And why was she in my bedroom?" Gus asked, sitting cuddled under his blankets.

"She is a witch who has many names depending on what country one is from. She is known as Mara, Night Hag, Boo Hag, but she is known more commonly as Nightmare. She attacks a sleeping person by sitting on them, forcing the air from their lungs, and causing fear to overcome her victims. She then feeds off the fear that she is creating in their dreams.

"Gus, this is not the first time she has been here! The slamming of the window confirmed it. Every time I had entered your room when you were screaming because of your bad dreams, the window would slam shut suddenly. She has been here all this time, Gus! Every nightmare, she has been here. But why? She does not usually single out one person so continuously. There are simply too many people on earth for that.

"She is up to something. My book also said that she was a concubine of the devil, that she takes her orders from him. Gus, this means that the devil may be after you," Molly said, her mind whirling.

"Quit trying to scare me! The devil is after everyone according to Reverend Rob," Gus said, trying not to be terrified.

Margie pushed against the large hinged wall. When she stepped through the opening, she found herself inside Grandma Bertie's barn. She rushed to the big sliding barn doors, opened them, and ran back to the blanket. With great effort, again Margie pulled Janice into the barn.

She was thrilled for Gus, Molly, and Grandma Bertie that Janice was safe and found. But if she went in and woke everyone up, then they would ask too many questions. "Where have you been? What were you doing? Why did you sneak out to go to the Shelter Tree at this hour? Where did you find Janice?" There would be just too many questions that she wanted no part in answering.

Margie checked Janice's pulse. *It is strong. I'll leave her here in the barn, then she'll be discovered in the morning. And I won't be the one answering questions.*

When Margie was satisfied that Janice was warm and as comfortable as possible, she headed toward the moonlight in Bertie's backyard and tiptoed toward the house and her opened window.

"I think I'll go check on Margie," Grandma Bertie said.

Just then, Margie appeared at the doorway. She was noticeably out of breath.

"What's goin' on?" Margie asked. "I heard screaming." Molly saw that Margie's hands looked filthy, like she had been digging in the dirt. Margie noticed and quickly put her hands behind her back. "Hold that thought. I have to go to the bathroom!" Margie backed into the hall and raced next door to the bathroom and locked the door behind her.

"Witches are real?" Gus stared blankly forward as he digested this new revelation. Grandma Bertie flopped down on the edge of Gus's bed; she looked white as a ghost. "Grandma, are you all right?" Gus asked, a little concerned. Bertie took a deep breath.

"I'll be fine. It's just a lot to take in all at once." She gasped. Molly was at the door, preoccupied with Margie's disappearance into the bathroom.

"Gus, of course witches are real. I am sure you remember who made the jack-o'-lantern," Molly scolded him, still looking at the bathroom door, waiting for Margie's return.

"Yeah, but that was a long time ago, and *that* witch is long gone, like the good presidents," Gus said.

Grandma Bertie began to cough uncontrollably as if she was choking on something. Molly looked at her and gauged the severity of Grandma Bertie's cough when the door to Margie's bedroom slammed shut.

"Darn it!" Molly cried.

Bertie got up and headed for the door. "'Cuse me, dear," Grandma Bertie managed to say, nudging by Molly toward the kitchen.

"Grandma, are you all right?" Molly asked as she followed her to the kitchen. Bertie filled a cup with water from the faucet and gulped down half of the glass of water and coughed one last time.

"Yes." She took another very deep breath. "I'm good. I'll be fine," she said, gaining her composure. Gus joined them in the kitchen.

"Can we have cookies 'n' milk? It will help calm my nerves so I can sleep," Gus asked sheepishly. Grandma Bertie smiled.

"Sure, that sounds like a great idea," Bertie said, still smiling. "Margie!" No sooner had she said her name when Margie was in her seat at the table ready for the midnight snack. Her hair was brushed, her pajamas were on, and her hands were clean. Molly was stewing in curiosity.

They were all dunking chocolate chip cookies into their milk when Grandma Bertie started a conversation.

"Kids, evil has many forms, and it is responsible for many terrible things that happen in this world—even death." Grandma

Bertie paused in thought momentarily. "We must be better prepared for the next attack."

"What do you mean next attack?" Gus squeaked.

"Evil is all around us every day, Gus. We simply don't see it.
We must be better prepared and guarded against it. I let down
my guard, and you were not prepared to fight against this night
witch," Bertie said, staring at the center of the table. "I had heard
an old wives' tale once when I was your age that said if you place
a broom in your bedroom at night that it will keep the night hag
busy 'til dawn and prevent nightmares. It seemed silly really, but
maybe there is some truth to it after all."

"Are you saying that you put the broom in Gus's bedroom on
purpose?" Molly asked.

"No, no, dear. I meant to clean that room a few days ago. I put
the broom down and never got back around to it. I must have
gotten preoccupied," Bertie said. "That reminds me, I want you
two to pick up all of your stuff so that I can sweep and dust this
week." Gus and Molly both made faces that screamed of torture.

"Aaaaww!" they said.

"Grandma, my messiness may have saved my life tonight. I don't
really feel comfortable with change right now," Gus countered.

"Dear, you are lucky that she could even see a broom underneath all of your clothes. With a clean room, a broom will be
more obvious to find. And I am very comfortable with that,"
Grandma Bertie said. Molly shook her head at Gus.

"Stop it, Molly! Grandma, tell her to quit making faces at me."

"I think it's time for bed," Grandma said, corralling the troops.

Looking up at Grandma Bertie, Gus grabbed the broom that
Grandma had brought into the kitchen. "Yes, you can have the
broom. Just clean your room in the mornin'. I think I might have
rolled my ankle again on a pile of your clothes," Bertie said, wincing in pain as she hobbled down the hall to put the kids to bed,
All except Molly, of course, who had once again stationed herself
on the couch in the front room.

Thanks to Gus's snoring, she had discovered that the couch was the most comfortable and quiet place in the house. His snoring was rivaled by Grandma Bertie's, and Margie cried herself to sleep most nights. Everyone had resettled in their places once again for the night.

Gus stared at the broom in the corner of his room, unsure if he could fall back to sleep with that thing still out there somewhere. Margie had closed and locked her door as usual. She made some notes in the ancient book, reviewing her favorite spell. She could hear Gus snoring two doors down. *It won't be long, mother, and we will be together again. I promise!* Tears began to flow down her cheeks.

Grandma Bertie was in deep thought; her mind was spinning, trying to bring the events of the evening to a conclusion. She again feared for her family's safety. She reached for an ancient book, hoping to calm her nerves. She read a couple of lines and closed the Bible and began to pray. Soon Margie heard Grandma snoring even louder than Gus.

Officer Sims struggled to the surface from deep beneath the water. He thought that he'd never get there. Once he broke through the waves, he suddenly woke up from a deep sleep, gasping for air. A green cloud vanished out the open passenger-side window unnoticed.

Officer Sims gathered his nerves and laid his head back and closed his eyes to rest for a brief moment. Soon he was snoring again, catching up on some needed sleep.

Jack had made his way back into the main hall; he sat on the large round table and thought as he looked at the remnants of the three dead henchmen. *One last task and then I'm free!*

Bertie dreamed of Steven that night. She woke the next morning well rested. Her night's journeys were still fresh in her mind; she lifted her Bible, and as she reached for the diary underneath, she felt a twinge of pain in her ankle. Lifting the covers, Bertie saw that her ankle was purple and swollen. She had already missed her first scheduled marathon because of a bone chip, and it looked like now she would be forced to miss another because of a sprain. She ignored her pain; she had too much to write before the kids woke up hungry for breakfast.

When Bertie finished writing in her journal, she placed the notebook back under her Bible. Now she was on a mission. The night's events had altered her plans for the day, and she needed Steven's help. He knew all of the best antiquing places in the state. He would know exactly where she needed to go to find what she wanted, and she was taking the kids with her.

Steven Grogan was watching the weather forecast in his bedroom as he dressed when the phone rang. It was Bertie. She asked if he could take her antiquing today with the kids. Steven had many yards to deal with and didn't see how he possibly could get away.

"I hear you, but I can't let a day or two of good weather go by without mowing as many lawns as I can. Actually, I was goin' to ask Gus if he could help me again today, Bertie. I just don't think I could go today," Steven said with a guilt streak running up his spine. He hated to disappoint Bertie.

"Well, would you change your mind if it started to rain?" Bertie asked.

"Um, sure Bertie, but I just saw the forecast, and it is supposed to be sunny for the next week." Steven listened for Bertie's response but heard what he thought sounded like thunder. He slid back the curtain on his bedroom window. Rain was streaming down outside.

"Well, what do you know! Bertie, you won't believe this, but it looks like we are goin' shoppin'." Steven hung up the phone in disbelief, shaking his head. Bertie put down the phone with a sigh of relief, and a childish grin grew upon her face as if she knew something that no one else did—and she wasn't telling a soul what it was. Gus, who had overheard her conversation, raised both of his fists in the air triumphantly, mouthing to the heavens, "Thank you."

Margie came into the kitchen yawning as Grandma Bertie hung up the phone. Bertie told everyone the plan. Margie felt ill.

"Grandma, don't you think we should stay and move those plants and trees from around the house to where we had planned by the barn today?"

"No, that can wait for a sunny day, dear. I need to do this today. It'll be fun. You'll see."

"Has anyone checked the hens in the barn for fresh eggs this morning?" Margie asked, looking at Gus.

"*No,*" Gus said, quite offended. "You go check them. It's pouring down rain out there." Margie huffed in frustration.

"Oh never mind!"

Bertie let them feed themselves that morning as she stretched and worked her ankle so that she could walk without pain. Gus and Molly very cheerfully downed two bowls of Captain Crunchies. Margie managed to ease down a small dish of yogurt with blueberries. Her nerves were on edge. She tried desperately to get someone to go outside to discover Janice Johnson lying in the barn. But no one was interested in getting wet. Her stomach churned with nausea over the situation.

Steven had driven his pickup to town to rent a car for the day; neither he nor Bertie had a vehicle large enough for five passengers. He came back in a new SUV that could seat eight.

Bertie was waiting impatiently for his return, which would have been much sooner had Steven been able to figure out how to start the new ride. The attendant finally came out and showed him how to insert the plastic computer chip key and turn it to start the engine. Even then, he could hardly hear the engine running. He realized that technology had surpassed him long ago.

When he finally arrived at Bertie's, she gave him an egg and sausage sandwich wrapped in plastic along with a glare that spoke for itself. Margie pointed toward the barn.

"Look, the barn doors are open," Margie said.

"Gus, would you mind closing them for me? I must have forgotten to close them last night," Bertie said, ready to leave.

Gus ran through the rain, pulled the doors together, and ran back to the SUV. Margie freaked.

"Gus, you didn't latch the door!" Margie said, percolating with annoyance when Gus failed to look inside to see his mother lying on the floor.

Margie ran through the rain to the barn. She cracked open the doors to peek inside. She couldn't see what she wanted, so she slid the doors to open them wider. The spot where she had left Janice was bare. She stepped in for a closer look. Margie searched everywhere quickly with her eyes. Finally, looking down where she had left Janice lying cozy under several blankets, she saw squiggly lines in the dirt but no Janice. *What happened? Where did she go? Where could she be? Now what do I do?*

"Margie, come on! Close the doors and come on!" Bertie yelled. Reluctantly, Margie slid the doors together. She climbed in, and they were off. She looked ill with worry, but no one noticed. They were focused on the road trip.

Steven had mapped out in his mind the route with the best scenery and sites that the kids had not had the privilege of knowing prior to the trip—Amish farm country.

Margie's mind and stomach were spinning. She closed her eyes and napped, hoping the stress of this nightmare morning would dissipate with more sleep. The rhythm of the rain helped soothe her nerves as she drifted to sleep.

She woke up when her head smacked into the window that she was using as a pillow as the SUV hit a pothole in the road. It was no longer raining; the sun was bright in the sky, warming her face through the glass. Margie had never seen so many trees outside of Willow Branch Forest. It reminded her of her favorite place in the whole world.

The roads that Steven took were narrow, winding, and slow, but even so, the passengers were jostled from side to side with every sharp turn. The three amigos in the backseats were hooked on the coolness of the trip once they passed the first horse-drawn buggy. The rolling farmland was littered with activity as boys of all ages in dark pants and light blue short-sleeve shirts under straw hats and girls wearing long plain dresses with bonnets tied under their chins picked the days ripened vegetables.

Margie, who had momentarily forgotten her plight, pointed out the window toward a white-bearded man, who was dressed similarly to the boys, walking behind a team of sturdy white horses with thick hair covering their hooves and dragging what Steven said was a cultivator.

"It is how they weed their fields."

The three of them in the backseats marveled that these people did not use modern equipment to do their work. It was like going back in time over a hundred and fifty years to early Americana.

Their three-and-a-half-hour ride did not seem so long with all of the sights. Gus was impressed with the farms and was thrilled that he at least did not have to mow grass with a handheld scythe as he had seen some doing. Molly loved looking at the animals, the workhorses being her favorite, but she was thrilled with all of the other livestock also. She had never seen so many cows, goats, or sheep in her life.

Margie enjoyed all of it because it took her mind away from the fact that she was now responsible for Gus and Molly's missing mother. But what struck her most were the rolling hills full of trees that they had passed through before entering the cleared-out farmlands of the Amish. They had reminded her of home and her mother, and it sparked a new sense of purpose for her this day, and for that she was excited.

"Oh look, kids." Grandma Bertie pointed to her left. "It looks like a barn raisin'."

Several men from neighboring farms had come together to help build a barn for a family in the community. It was a common practice for these people to assist one another; their community was like a large family. Often, a community actually was an extended family by blood relations or by marriage.

They saw a skeleton of thick wooden beams notched together, like Gus's Lincoln Logs that he used to play with when he was younger, down a long, narrow gravel driveway across from a white two-story farmhouse. Men were walking across the thick wooden beams as others hoisted up another crossbeam.

The car slowed down and turned right away from the action onto a long winding paved drive through a pasture where cows roamed freely that led to a grouping of three newer-looking large buildings. Steven parked in the designated area under a monstrous oak tree that shaded the entire area to the store. A large red barn with an arching roof had a sign above a wide doorway opening that read Guest Relations and Country Store.

A banner flew high between the red barn and a much more modern looking pole barn that had Cafeteria painted on the side facing the road. The banner read Amish Antique and Craft Fair. Gus, Margie, and Molly walked under the banner and stood facing the chaos toward the back of the property while Steven and Grandma Bertie entered the store.

They saw a field of rolling green grass with a couple of small barns and people everywhere milling about in every direction. Venders' booths were set up in a circular pattern around a large pond located in the middle of all the activity. They could hear music playing in the distance while mimes and jugglers mingled with the crowd near the entrance. Gus and Molly were all smiles. This looked like a fun place, and it possessed the sounds of excitement. Margie was in awe of it all as Grandma Bertie and Steven joined them with tickets and maps for everyone.

"Okay, there is tons to see here today, and I will let you three go by yourselves, but you must stay together. We will meet back at the cafeteria at one thirty. Okay? Great. Have fun." Steven and Bertie gave their tickets to the attendant and headed to the left around the pond. The threesome decided to go in the opposite direction.

They had three hours to kill before they would meet again to eat at the cafeteria barn. The staff at the reception area, the gift shop, and the cafeteria had consisted of local Amish folks. The venders, however, in their 10' × 10' tents were from all over the country. Each tent had a small cardboard sign with the booth's name, the vender's name(s), and the place where they were from. Gus stepped into a Native American art booth that was actually authentic. "Cindy 'Singing Pass' Meadows from Alberta, Canada," the sign read. He marveled at the detailed paintings, beaded accessories, and turquoise jewelry.

Cindy saw him staring at a painting of an Aspen Forest; white trees with yellow leaves filled the canvas. It was beautifully lifelike.

"Do you see the wolves?" she asked him as she came to his side. Curious, Margie and Molly joined Gus to see what he was looking at.

"There are seven wolves hidden within the trees," Cindy said.

They all focused on the painting but could see nothing of a single wolf. And then they began to come into focus, one and then another and another until finally they had discovered all seven.

"Wow! How cool was that?" Gus beamed, turning toward his sisters. "That was awesome! Thank you," he said, now looking at Cindy. "I think I am going to try that again."

He turned back toward the painting; the wolves had again hidden themselves in the white, grey, and black bark of the trees. Then, as slowly as before, they began to reappear.

They looked at many fun and interesting booths, but some were quite boring or repetitive. They found three different venders selling leather wristbands with names engraved along the strap. Molly was the first to discover her name among hundreds scattered on a table that had probably been in alphabetical order earlier that morning but was now a heap of leather.

They scouted out several more booths along the outer rim of the pond but decided not to purchase anything until after seeing all of the booths and then going back later to pick out what they truly wanted. Gus wanted to buy the wolf painting, but it was priced at $345, slightly out of his budget of $56. He didn't like the plan to wait before buying, but after finding things that caught his eye in seven out of the fifteen tents that they visited, he realized that it might not be such a bad idea.

Once they had seen all of the displays on the outer rim of the pond, they decided to circle back on the inner rim nearest to the pond. Gus, Margie, and Molly found many booths filled with glass knickknacks, fake flowers, music by local musicians, antique books, and country crafts made of wood. They grew tired of dodging slower pedestrians while not buying anything and decided to rest under a shade tree by the pond and listen to the minstrels by the water's edge.

Grandma Bertie on the other side of the pond was dragging Steven from booth to booth, looking for some specific items but finding nothing she wanted. And then she saw what she was looking for. The booth sold wooden furniture, vine wreaths, and old-fashioned wooden-handled brooms. Some were fixed with cinnamon bristles and were just for show, but Bertie found some that were functional as tools for sweeping with balsam fir bristles. This was exactly what she had been searching for. Bertie picked through a stack of ten sitting in the back corner of the tent.

"Here, hold these," she said, handing two to Steven for safe-keeping. *One for each bedroom. That's three. Oh and one for the living room for Molly makes four.* She handed Steven two more brooms. He had a puzzled look on his face, but he did not dare to ask questions. Bertie then looked at him as if she had just remembered something.

"Do you have a broom at home?"

"No, but I—"

"Five," she said and gave him another broom.

We drove all this way for brooms? I'm sure that Hillmart carries quality brooms, but I had better not say so.

"Now we need to find a vender that deals with dried herbs. So keep your eyes peeled."

They searched each tent, zigzagging the walking path, marveling at the people there, and soaking up the warm sun. And then she smelled its fragrance before she saw the bundle of dried lavender hanging from the corners of one tent. This was the place where she would find what she needed.

The rain had gradually increased back in Willow Branch throughout the morning hours; now it was a total downpour. Liam O'Toole had slept in until 10:15 a.m.; he had been up all night, waiting for word back from his employees that he sent out on a special errand. It was only after one thirty in the morning that he had finally been informed that three-fourths of his crew was missing. At twelve thirty, he drove through the downpour to his office at the lumber yard. He considered calling the local police chief to report his concern, but he decided to wait and see if they showed up at the office in the morning before taking needless precautions.

He was not concerned about the welfare of the missing workers. He was concerned whether they had achieved their assignment or not. *How hard could it be to kill an eleven-year-old in her sleep?* His black dually truck with an extended cab pulled through the mud to the stoop of his trailer office.

The short, fat man fumbled with his keys, searching for the one marked Office on the grip covered in clear tape. He turned the knob and pushed through the doorway and leaned against the door to close it against the wind. He shook off the wet and hung his raincoat on the coat-tree next to the door. He turned, and his back was driven into the door by what he saw on the opposite side of the room.

Three grotesque figures stared at him from the sofa. Two were shriveled to the bone and looked like grey dried-out, mummified bodies with hollowed eyes. The third was charred black and carried the worst stench Liam had ever smelled. He tugged his mobile phone from his pants pocket. His hands shook uncontrollably; he had to redial three times before the fat man finally managed to tap out the correct number.

"C-C-Chief? Y-Your mummifying murderer has struck again. Y-You need to get over here now!" He did not wait for an answer; when he finished speaking, he pressed the End button on his phone. The owner of the Cutter Logging Company and the lumber yard inched forward to take a closer look at the dead bodies. "What in hell happened to you?"

"Hell had nothing to do with it!" Liam spun around to see the glowering eyes and mouth of the jack-o'-lantern as it slid from behind the clothes tree by the door. The fat man tripped, falling backward onto the bodies of his dead employees. He was filled with terror as he struggled to get up off the dead, stinking corpses as the creature came toward him. "I must thank you. You just made my task much easier."

"No, no, wait, please!"

"It's too late for that, boyo. Your time is up! You should never have messed with the witch's family. This is for Margie's mother."

Lightning flashed through the trailer's window, illuminating a vine gripping the fat man's throat with terror on his face. The jack-o'-lantern's shadow eclipsed his face as the creature vanquished his light forever.

"No!"

Gus, Margie, and Molly had circled the entire fair around the pond and were sitting crouched along the side of the cafeteria barn, waiting as Steven appeared carrying five brooms and three bags. Grandma Bertie was trailing close behind holding a large bag in each hand.

"Who's hungry?" Bertie asked. All three answered.

"Me!"

"Nobody bought anything?" Bertie's brow pinched together as she stood slightly disappointed and in disbelief. "Okay, well get in line, and we'll put this stuff in the back of the car."

They did as they were told. The line moved quickly; they had missed the rush from 11:00 a.m. to 1:00 p.m., but the seating inside was still packed. Gus and Margie found a spot along the back wall with plenty seats. Bertie gave the lunch tickets to the clerk while Steven and Molly carried three trays of hamburgers, fries, and drinks to the table.

After lunch, it was time to buy. Gus had his eyes on a collection of baseball cards that he was sure was worth much more than what he was about to pay. Molly saw a cute sea-green dragon marionette that she thought was a necessity, and Margie was after a very large very old ornate family Bible that she had seen at an antique book tent.

Steven and Bertie, who followed them on the afternoon buying spree around the pond, were surprised by Margie's purchase. Margie had never shown any interest in church or the Bible before, and this version was going to set her back $150. They did not want to discourage her interest now; besides, it was her money to spend. Well, the money that she had taken from Carl's secret stash was finally coming in handy today.

Steven lugged her Bible with both of his mammoth hands as they headed back to the car. It was 4:00 p.m. by the time they started the trek back to Willow Branch. They expected to be back before nightfall. Everyone looked to the right in amazement as they passed a completely finished barn that was bigger than Grandma Bertie's. Several men on ladders were putting on the finishing coat of white paint.

"Is that the same one from this morning?" Gus asked.

"Amazin', isn't it?" Grandma Bertie replied. No one said a word; they just watched in awe as they continued down the road toward home.

A police car pulled up behind the black Ram dually parked next to the front door of the Cutter Logging Company trailer office. Thunder and lightning crashed and danced across the Willow Branch skyline, but the rain had finally let up to a light drizzle as Chief O'Reilly stepped out of his car onto the puddle-laden driveway of stone. His pistol was pulled. He opened the front door with extreme caution.

"Liam?"

It was dark; the light switch did not work when he flicked it. *Power must still be out.* Officer O'Reilly wished he could have involved his deputies as backup as he reached to his utility belt for his flashlight.

He had known Liam O'Toole since his school days at Willow Branch Junior High. O'Toole had always been a bully. He was a son of alcoholic parents who seemed to fight for entertainment. Liam had known violence in his home since he could remember. And he seemed to have an affinity for it.

He was shorter that most of his classmates, but he was thick and strong when he was younger. He was like a wolverine; he would fight anyone no matter how big they were. He knew no fear.

O'Reilly remembered that he got his start at middle line-backer in high school when O'Toole, who had been teased by Johnny Harris, the school's only all-state football player, punched Johnny in the side, fracturing two ribs and puncturing his left lung. "You're up, Irish! Make the most of it," he said as he walked past O'Reilly in the hall, voluntarily on his way to the office to receive his inevitable expulsion.

Chief O'Reilly never knew Liam to show any signs of fear in all of his experiences with him. He heard the sound of someone's quivering voice on the phone earlier; he was not sure with whom he was speaking. When he realized it was Liam O'Toole, a pang of fear rippled throughout Chief O'Reilly. The chief drove over immediately, unsure of what he was going to find but expecting the worst.

A beam of condensed light from his flashlight lit up the name-plate on the messy desk that read Liam O'Toole. He smelled something coming from inside the trailer that nearly made him puke. It was the distinct odor of burned flesh. He had witnessed burn victims on occasion when working with the fire department over the years.

"Liam?"

Chief O'Reilly pushed open the door. Death was staring him in the face. Four bodies were piled onto the sofa on the opposite wall from the door. He wasn't sure but he thought the short one lying on top was what used to be Liam O'Toole, the nastiest man in Willow Branch. He stepped closer to examine the bodies.

He wasn't sure because of their shriveled condition but he thought they were Liam, Bubba, Danny, and Chester. He couldn't remember their last names though he knew them; they had been Liam's employees that doubled as his muscle of influence. He used them to bully, coerce, or bribe people to better his business opportunities.

Half of Willow Branch would cheer his death as they felt freedom from his bondage of blackmail. Liam had something on every elected official and most of the attorneys in town. Chief O'Reilly felt a momentary sense of relief as he looked upon their deformed bodies. Liam had plenty of unscrupulous dirt on Sergeant O'Reilly as well. The brief moment passed, and he was left in shock, wondering who or what could have done this to them.

The door slammed shut behind him. Chief O'Reilly spun in response. It was now completely dark except for his narrow beam of light. He saw nothing. He began to breathe again as he dropped his shoulders and sighed. Pulling a handkerchief from his back pocket, he placed it over his nose and mouth. The stench from Bubba's burned body was too much for him.

He turned back toward the bodies on the sofa.

"Finally, my secret dies with you, you foul son of—"

"I don't think so," a deep rasping voice interrupted. Officer O' Reilly spun, looking up into the eyes of the harbinger of death, the jack-o'-lantern. His eyes blazed with hate. "I know your dirty little secret. You murdered Melinda Dunn! She swerved to miss a car driving on the wrong side of the road that night. Fat man's flunkies could not drive fast enough in the company truck to catch her and push her off the edge of the cliff. You were coming to save the day and stop them, but you were the reason she ran off the road, and Liam knew it and held it over your head to do as he wished. And it will cost you dearly!"

Chief O'Reilly pulled the radio from his shoulder harness with his left hand and drew his sidearm with his right, and he shot at the creature. "Need backup now at Cutter's" was all he could get out before he succumbed to his fate.

"Justice is served, my lady." Sirens screamed in the distance as Jack disappeared into the rain.

Gus was the last one out of bed Sunday morning. He finally made his way to Bertie's round kitchen table, where his sisters and Grandma Bertie were glued to the breaking news on the local news broadcast on channel seven.

"Thank you, Lisa. Shocking news this morning. Patrick O'Reilly, the chief of police in Willow Branch, was found dead yesterday evening along with Liam O'Toole, proprietor of Cutter Logging and Mill, and three others, who were gruesomely disfigured, sources say. Police have given no details in this tragedy, but an anonymous source claims that this case may be linked to four other unsolved murders that took place some months ago. Stay tuned as we continue to follow this story that has Willow Branch on needles. For *Channel 7 News*, I'm Christie Clark. Back to you, Lisa."

Grandma Bertie turned the television off, and they all sat with glazed looks for the longest time without saying a word. Steven knocked and came in the side door to the kitchen.

"Did you hear the news?"

Bertie nodded.

They finished breakfast in silence. The news of the five that were found dead was shocking as the reporter had said, but they all knew what had killed them, and it had Janice hidden somewhere. Not even Margie knew if she was still alive or dead like the others. They all had heavy hearts as they headed to church and entered the arched, vastly ornate oak doors of Willow Branch Episcopal Church.

Reverend Robert "Rob" O'Reilly stood at the pulpit; he had been a pastor for twenty-five years. He had followed his father and his father's father before him into the ministry. He never regretted being a priest in this congregation until today.

Today, Rob did not feel prepared to deliver the eulogy that he had planned for this day. He wished that he could join the people in the pews, but here he stood before them with a heavy heart, feelings that he knew his congregation shared with him. He spoke of his brother Patrick, and their childhood. Reverend O'Reilly told how Patrick had chosen a different path but a noble path in life, protecting the people of Willow Branch.

"Today, in my sorrow, I want to bring him back and tell him how much I love him. It's a phrase I feel that I did not use often enough with my brother. But I can't bring my brother back. He's gone, and it isn't right for me or anyone of us to wish him back. His time here is over. He has moved on, and we must accept that—for our sake, our sanity, not those that pass before we do.

"When as believers we are dead and have gone to our Lord's side in heaven, will we want to return because those we left behind are sad, in grief, or are guilty with how they treated us and wish us back to make amends?" He scanned the audience thoughtfully.

"In Luke 16:19–31, we read that upon his death, Lazarus is at Abraham's side. He's in heaven and is comforted. He is at peace. And even if we wanted him to return, he cannot because there is a great chasm between him and us." He paused for a moment as he paced across the stage.

"Are we sad? Yes. Will we miss our loved ones? Yes. But we must move forward because that's what *life* is about. We must ready ourselves. We must be prepared for when our days are done, and we must give an account for our days. And when that day comes, there is no coming back.

"Matthew 12:36, 37 and 2 Corinthians 5:10 tell us this very thing: that we all must be prepared and we will be blessed or condemned based upon the words of our lips. So I ask you all today, are you ready? If not, will you choose today to be reconciled to God? He wants you to be with him forever—the choice he leaves up to you. Will you stand as we sing?"

Margie's heart sank, and her head was spinning in thought; she had never heard these words before, and now they were causing a war of ideas inside her head. She looked visibly ill. Grandma

Bertie put her to bed when they got home. Margie looked up the verses again in her new gigantic Bible. "Chasm, comforted by Abraham's side."

She searched her backpack and found a pocketknife that had belonged to Carl. She flipped through the large Bible to the first book of Samuel. Carefully, she carved a rectangle out of the middle of each page until she reached the book of Psalms. When she had finished, a deep vault was created; she pulled out the notebook pages that she had copied from the *Book of Spells* and placed them secretly inside the hidden compartment for safekeeping.

The Bible barely fit into her backpack as it lay on her bed; she slid the straps over her shoulders and heaved herself upright. She hobbled over to her window, crawled out, and ran through the backyard unnoticed. Inside the hollow of the Shelter Tree, Margie sat hugging her backpack for hours. She sat up, took a deep breath, and opened the trapdoor under the tree.

Once inside, she placed the Bible that she had wrapped in a grain sack from Bertie's barn and placed it in the same location under the root that had given her a knot on her head upon her first visit below the Shelter Tree. She scanned the cavern quickly before deciding that she had better get home before she was missed, and she left.

Jack watched her in secret as she ascended up the ramp. He slithered over to where she had been and lifted the heavy sack from its perch. He pulled the heavy book from its protective covering and opened it up. Flipping through the pages, he found the hollowed-out spot where she had stuffed her copies of the spells that she had written in pink and purple ink. Jack was encouraged that Margie was preparing for their next and all-important meeting set for Saturday. *Six days*, he thought, *six more days and I will be free!*

He flipped the pages past the Psalms and into the section labeled New Testament. Then a deep raspy voice inside his hollowed-out gourd shouted.

"What are you doing? I feel that faint flicker of hope that still resides in you raising its ugly head again. Well, I'm taking command of this ship back as of now."

"No," Jack burst. "I have let you bully me long enough. I am sick of being dragged around while you kill for your master."

"You forget yourself, Jacky. It was not me who the girl had kill for her. That was you! You are the guilty one, Jacky. And soon you too will finally pay dearly for your actions."

"Then let me be until then! I'm not giving you control."

"Hahaha! You will, Jacky! You will soon enough." The rasping demonic voice subsided, and Jack was alone with his thoughts— and with the open pages of the Bible before him.

He flipped through its pages aimlessly, stopping occasionally in the book of John, briefly reading 3:16, 17, and then he flipped some more, stopping at the chapter 15, and read verse 13 over and over. Jack again scanned a few pages as he skipped to the end of the gargantuan book. He found three more books written by an author named John; again he read 3:16 in the first of the three smaller books. When he had reread it, he slammed the book shut and left it sitting next to him on the round table in the center of the underground chamber as he brooded.

Janice Johnson opened her eyes. Everything was a bright blur swimming around her. Gradually, they adjusted to the newness of the light as the powerful sedative that she had been given nightly by the jack-o'-lantern finally faded from her system. She had no idea where she was or how she had gotten there. It was like she woke from a very bad dream only to find that the dream was real.

She was lying on a table in the center of the house of shattered glass. Janice was zipped inside of a thick sleeping bag. She was still very weak and could barely move her head to take in the full view of her nightmare. Through the glass house, she could see hundreds of pumpkins surrounding the house and filling the yard. She tried to yell for help, but her voice was too weak. She could see another house close-by, but it may as well have been a hundred miles away because Janice could not feel her limbs. She was hidden from the world by an eight-foot-tall fence to the rear and six-foot-tall grass at the front of the property. She was alone. She could hold her head up no longer and drifted back out of consciousness.

An orange pumpkin planted at the head of the table where she slept rose from its nest one limb at a time as it pulled itself upright next to her slumbering body. It had risen the previous night and was alerted by the night hag that, located in a barn not far away, lay the sacrifice that would feed Satan's army's initial attack upon Willow Branch.

It found her and brought her here for safekeeping until the others were finally ready. The pumpkin head reached out its arm of vine, extended a black thorn from it, and pierced Janice's neck for a bit of refreshment and to keep her out for a while longer.

The week before school started back up had been a stressful one. Willow Branch was buzzing with fear over the recent murders. The police department still had no clear leads or motives behind the terrible mutilations.

Though Officer Sims had been on the job for less than a year, he found himself as Chief O'Reilly's replacement with a staff that had been cut in half. Four in the department with seniority over Sims had transferred out of Willow Branch immediately after the chief's demise, leaving him in charge with three part-time retired officers for support. Their duties had consisted of meeting at the local donut shop to gather the morning gossip and then drive around town occasionally, visiting the stores along Main Street to chat with the owners until finally meeting for lunch. They were not exactly the crime-solving heroes that Chief Sims now found himself in desperate need of in the midst of the town's worst crisis in over a hundred years.

———————

Grandma Bertie had stayed away from town purposefully to avoid all of the rumors and fearmongering that was everywhere. But unfortunately for her, she needed to get the kids school clothes, and Molly had been in her ear all week about the school supplies that she needed to have this year. On the Friday before school started, she relented and took them all to town.

Molly had been driving them all bonkers all week. She was going into eighth grade and had been so bored during the final week before school that she was nearly bursting with joy for school to begin. She wanted the diversion that school provided her so that she could take her mind off her mother. Gus would have said that she had lost her mind, but he had seen this Molly every year the week before school began for seven years now; it was an annoyance but not a surprise to him at all.

Gus was torn. He really did not want school to begin as much as he wanted football to begin so that he would not have to mow any more yards for Steven. They had one more bank-owned property in the neighborhood to do, and it promised to be their last job together. His first practice game was scheduled for Saturday morning at nine, and then he would meet Steven for an all-day attack on a one-house job for the bank. But Gus was comforted that this job would definitely be his last.

———————

Margie had been more reserved than usual, distant and deep in thought all week. She enjoyed learning, but she hated the raucous, juvenile attitudes of her classmates, especially the ones who looked at her as if she were a freak and picked on her constantly. But her mind was not even registering her coming aggravation; she was struggling with something far more important to her. She was thinking about her mother and if she could go through with what she had planned for so long.

Grandma Bertie had tried talking with her on more than one occasion during the week, but Margie gave her short vague answers every time that she asked what was bothering her. She was concerned but assumed that it was something that Margie felt that she had to figure out on her own. Bertie had to repeat herself again to Margie as they stood looking at a rack of jeans at Save-More Department Store.

"Margie, do you like this shirt and have you picked out a pair of jeans that you want to try on?" Margie looked at Grandma Bertie as if she had just woken up from a deep sleep. Taking a deep breath, she responded, shaking her head at the shirt choice.

"I have these two pairs of jeans to try," she said without conviction.

"Black? Could you get at least one pair of blue jeans?" Bertie received a cold look. "Fine, fine, as long as you will wear them. That's all that really matters."

She shook her head as Margie went into the changing room. As Molly emerged with an arm full of brightly colored shirts and two pairs of skinny jeans, Bertie marveled at how different each grandchild was. She scanned the store, looking for Gus, who was supposed to find jeans of his own, but she found him empty-handed in the sporting goods section checking out the football toss display.

He met Bertie's scowl with a big smile.

"Grandma! Come watch me! I just made seven out of ten passes! Watch. I know I can do better."

She reluctantly watched as her temper subsided. She could never stay mad at him very long. She actually cheered when he made the eighth pass out of ten on his last toss.

"Okay, now go over to the boys' department and try on some jeans please."

"Sure! I'll be right back!" he said as he sped away.

Bertie was standing again in the girls' section with Molly by her side when Lisa Madas, the town's biggest gossip, saw Bertie and came over to chat.

"Oh, isn't this awful. No one is safe anymore. Have you heard the latest?" she said and continued without waiting for a reply. "The school board is going to have an emergency meeting tonight to decide whether to postpone the school year until the police catch whoever did this."

"Oh no," Molly said.

"Don't worry, dear. I am sure cooler heads will prevail and the school will open as usual."

Molly looked unsure.

"Aren't you on the school board, Lisa?" Bertie did not wait for her to respond. "So I am sure that you will lead the push for the school to start as it normally does so that we can begin some sense of normalcy again, even in the midst of these terrible times. Let's let the authorities handle this and believe that the one responsible for these deaths will eventually receive his due penalty. Am I right? Of course. I know that we can count on you and your voice of reason in this situation tonight, Lisa. Now if you'll excuse me, I must go round up my grandson. It was nice chatting with you."

Bertie walked away, leaving Lisa dazed as she considered what Bertie had insinuated. Lisa's eyes met Molly's for a brief moment, still in shock. Molly quickly dropped her gaze and went in the dressing room to check on Margie.

Gus had picked out three pairs of athletic shorts, one pair of jeans, and four T-shirts with Bertie's help. The kids were standing near the glass entrance's front doors as Grandma Bertie paid the cashier when Christie Clark and her *Channel 7 News* camera crew burst through the front doors.

A bright light beamed, blinding Margie as the reporter stuck a microphone in her face.

"Is it true that you, Margie Dunn, are the daughter of Carl Hughes, who was brutally murdered in your presence, and that the murderer had abducted you before you were found lying in the middle of the road?"

"Carl's not my father!" Margie yelled.

"Leave her alone," Molly said as Gus stepped in front of Margie.

"Can you give us any clue as to who this murderer might be or what he looked like?"

"What is going on here?" Bertie cried. "What is wrong with you people? Leave us alone! And turn that thing off!" she said, pushing the camera out of her face as she led the children out the door and to her red-and-white Ford.

As Bertie sped home, she called Chief Sims to keep the news crews from harassing her and her family. The media in town were eating up the disaster ratings like the vultures on the national broadcasts usually do even if they have to create the disaster themselves.

Chief Sims was an overwhelmed officer of the law, but he guaranteed Bertie that she would not have any more trouble. He could not, however, guarantee Bertie a quick resolution to this growing crisis.

When Steven came over for dinner, Bertie was still seething. He listened intently to their stories of the day as they ate. Later, when they were playing cards at the kitchen table as the three kids played badminton in the backyard, Steven tried to assure her, but she was caught up in the dread of the situation.

"Maybe they should close the schools."

"Until when? Bertie, you were right. We can't hide simply because bad things are happening. We must continue to live our lives. We must live each day with our faith in God's sovereignty and provision. If we don't, then we have already begun to die." She sat for the longest time before she looked him in the eyes and nodded.

It was half past ten before the grandchildren were ready for bed. Bertie tucked them all in. Even Molly on the front room couch had her very own balsam fir broom leaning up against the fireplace to keep the nightmare away. Bertie had one for every bedroom; even Steven had to promise her that he had his next to the bed. Bertie believed what Steven had said about trusting God, but she was taking no chances with this situation. She was determined to do all she could to keep them all safe.

She had made them all necklaces and wristbands of buckthorn and sweet bay with the herbs that she purchased at the Amish fair. An old book on herb lore claimed that sweet bay protected against witches and the devil. Buckthorn was known to drive away enchantments and sorceries.

Steven again had to promise her that he would wear it even though he felt it was unnecessary and foolish; he held his tongue and appeased her. They all slept soundly that night except for Bertie and Margie. They had too many thoughts whirling through their minds to fully settle into a sound sleep.

———

The Mara returned to Lantern Street that night. She peered into Gus's window but saw the broom of balsam fir in the corner, which she knew would prevent her from entering his room successfully. The girl that she was ordered to monitor was not yet asleep. She floated her way toward the opened door of the barn before she noticed that balsam fir was hanging above the door, preventing her to move any closer. She saw a woman lying inside asleep, but she could not reach her safely. Mara hissed as she turned and left. She made her way through the neighborhood, stopping to check in on the growth and ripeness of the pumpkin army. She surveyed them quickly and headed back to her master.

"My lord, the vessels are ready for the transfer." The devil nodded.

"Excellent! Then this day will be my glory with the beginning of the end of creation! Send Death to the earth through the door in Willow Branch! And I will have my revenge with my pumpkin army." Satan gleamed as he greedily gnashed his teeth.

A spotty fog invaded the valley town of Willow Branch on Saturday morning. After his usual breakfast with Bertie, Steven kissed her and set out to tackle his last bank-owned property. Bertie could hardly see his headlights as he pulled his truck and trailer out of his driveway across the road.

Gus woke up at 8:30 a.m. He was supposed to be at the school dressed and stretching at the football field by 8:35 a.m. He grabbed a piece of toast and a couple of pieces of bacon as he rushed out the door at a full sprint.

"Good luck! And have fun!" Bertie yelled as the door slammed behind Gus. She slid open the back door and rejoined Margie and Molly with transplanting some flowers around her house. They had been up since 7:30 a.m. and had already split and moved several hostas to their new home around the perimeter of the barnv.

The mist kissed their faces as they moved back and forth from the house to the barn. Stale air met Grandma Bertie as she opened the barn doors to search for a large container that she needed for a seedling that she was going to dig up. It had made a home next to the base of her house and needed to be moved to a more appropriate place for it to flourish and not tear up the foundation of the house. She left the doors open to air out the barn, and she made her way back to the seedling.

"How are we doing, girls? About ready for a break?"

"No, I'm having too much fun," Molly said.

"Well, you two can finish the hostas and then tackle the pruning of the roses if you wish. I am goin' to get my hair cut, then I'll be back to help you. I won't be gone long."

"Bye!" Margie and Molly cheered.

They continued to work, digging, cutting, and planting. Molly stood up after she transplanted the final hosta and brushed the dirt off her knees and gloves and then pushed the hair from her face as she observed her handiwork.

"I have to go to the bathroom, Margie. Do you want me to bring you something to drink when I come back?"

"Lemonade?"

"Sure. I'll be right back!"

Margie worked diligently, planting the oak seedling in a sunny spot in the corner of the yard. She looked to see if Molly was coming back with the lemonade. *No sign of her.* Margie jogged to the barn and pulled the hidden wall open in Bertie's barn. She pulled out a flashlight that she had stashed inside her jacket pocket and clicked on the beam of light. She glanced back over her shoulder toward the house to make sure Molly was not watching and entered the cobweb-filled corridor. Margie heaved to pull the door shut behind her but it did not seal tightly and crept open slightly.

Molly was in the kitchen, pouring lemonade, when she saw Margie enter the barn. She came outside, looking to hand Margie the glass of lemonade, but Margie was nowhere to be found. Molly went to the barn but did not see her there either. She turned to go back to the kitchen when she noticed that the sidewall was cracked open like a door.

Molly pulled it farther open and looked inside. She saw the large rusted hinges on the inside that made the hidden door secretly look like a wall. *Wow. Cool, I wonder if Grandma knows that she has a secret door in the wall of her barn.*

Molly ran back to the kitchen to set the glasses of lemonade in the refrigerator and found a flashlight. She raced back to the opened door. *I wonder why Margie went exploring without me. Well, I am going to find out what she is up to.* An unnerving shiver went up Molly's spine as her hand swiped away cobweb after cobweb as she made her way deeper and deeper into the underground tunnel.

Steven slowed his truck and trailer to a complete stop in front of a mailbox that dangled from a single bent nail that clung to the post in front of a house with a yard that featured a jungle of six-foot-tall grass. Steven sighed as he slid out of the cab and turned to look over the job from the street. He walked to the back of his trailer, put down the tailgate, and rolled down his orange DR brush mower.

It was his go-to machine for unruly yards with outrageously tall lawns and/or weeds. It could even mow over small-diameter trees. The DR had a mowing deck out front with two thick, knobby, rubber tires and with handlebars where the operator walked behind as the mower propelled itself. It was Steven's favorite toy.

He pushed the choke switch, turned the key, and the engine coughed then fired up. He switched the choke lever to neutral again and pulled up the power take-off knob. The blades began to hum. Steven pushed the gear speed lever to 1, which was better suited for heavy workloads, and squeezed the throttle with his left hand that rested on the handle bar, propelling the DR toward its prey. The grass toppled to the ground as Steven followed the mower along the fence at the front of the yard.

Gus had made it to the field dressed and ready to play with five minutes to spare before the nine o'clock kickoff. Coach Sturm gave Gus the evil eye when Gus showed up at warm-ups. Gus sat out the first quarter as punishment for being late, and then he was allowed to enter the second quarter on the third play of the drive.

He came into the huddle with a play that was designed to go to the fullback up the middle; they needed nine yards for the first down, but Gus decided that the coach needed to learn to call a better game since the big fat kid playing nose tackle was making all of the tackles for the other team. So he called his own number for a sweep around left end, right in front of his team's bench and within shouting distance of the coach.

The quarterback surveyed the defense and barked out the cadence. "Blue 32. Blue 32. Set. Hut, hut." The quarterback dropped back, faked the handoff to the fullback and pitched the ball underhand to Gus as he sprinted for the left corner.

Coach Sturm was yelling obscenities at Gus as he swooshed past him down the sidelines. Gus smiled and yelled back, "Touchdown!" The fog was thick at the opponent's end of the field. Gus ran his hardest, but it seemed like the end zone would never arrive. He could hear the footsteps of his would-be tacklers close behind as he entered a thicker patch of fog.

Gus wondered if the referees could even see him as he neared the goal line. Finally, he crossed the line for a score; his team eventually found him and pounced on him in celebration. Upon reaching the sidelines, Coach Sturm informed him that he was free to go home early.

"That's not necessary, Coach. I am ready to play all day!"

It was the look that Coach Sturm had that gave Gus the clue that it was not an optional perk of his great run but rather a punishment for making the coach look good but showing him up in the process.

Gus slunk away from the team, disappearing into the fog at the other end of the field. As he walked, his depression mounted upon his back and grew with each step that he took closer to the house with the mile-high grass. He now had to help Steven with this monster of a yard.

Gus, still wearing his football pants and cleats and carrying his helmet and shoulder pads, made his way through the neighborhood and onto the train tracks. Visions of a scene from his past flashed before him as he plodded down the tracks.

He was retracing his steps. He could see the church steeple at a distance, and then he was lying facedown on the tracks, and the creature was close behind. Out of nowhere, the train hit as Gus dove into the ditch that ran along the railway. And the vision was over.

Gus realized that he was in the same ditch in front of the same fence as before, and he wondered how long he had walked enchanted with the reliving of the worst day of his life. He stood at the base of a fence, the fence where he had been before, even in his dreams. He dreaded heading around to the front; he hated to mow and knew that this would be an all-day task. But he pushed himself forward only for Steven's sake.

When Grandma Bertie returned home with her refreshed do of short silver spiky hair, she found no one home. She made her way to the barn to see if they were playing in the hayloft when she discovered the opened sidewall.

"Oh no!" Her heart skipped a beat. "Oh dear, what have they done?" Bertie grabbed a flashlight from inside the house and ran back to the barn. She stepped into the corridor for the first time in years.

Margie stepped from the corridor into the great room of the cavern beneath the Shelter Tree. Jack was sitting on the round table, waiting for her.

"Glad you decided to join me, my dear," he hissed, holding a large book in his gnarly vine hands. She recognized it as her *Book of Spells*. *How did he get that?* "I assume by now that you have heard the news that I carried out your wishes as you commanded."

"The chief?"

"Yes, I must admit that I, too, was taken aback by this discovery. Intentional or not, he was the one at fault and did indeed cover it up, with the logging company taking the fall though without any evidence to back it up, well, let's just say that it was a short drop. However, they still saw you as a threat, one worthy of getting rid of, so it seems that you beat them to the punch." His voice echoed throughout the chamber as Margie moved closer to him.

Margie was visibly shaking. It was cool underground, but her trembling came from her cold feet not her cold blood. She stared at the ground, unable or unwilling to look into his flaming eyes.

"I… I can't do this."

"What do you mean?" The jack-o'-lantern asked. "We made a deal! Blood has been spilled. Don't you know what that means? There is no going back. You owe a debt—and it will be paid!" Jack bellowed as flames shot out from his mouth.

"I knew she would not go through with it!" another voice screamed from within the flaming skull of the jack-o'-lantern.

This voice was deep and rasping—evil. "I made a provision for such an event, and here he comes now." The viney arm pointed to the far wall behind them.

Down, beneath Margie's secret hideaway, in the cavern that used to shelter runaway slaves during the Civil War, there was a place that Jack Smythe, the man cursed into the form of a jack-o'-lantern, called home. Now, there stood Satan himself. Jack had the *Book of Spells* and the witch, who he had promised to Satan in return for everlasting life as a human.

"Here they are. I have upheld my end of the bargain. Now grant me my eternal wish as you have promised in exchange," Jack said, glaring at the devil.

"You tricked me!" Margie yelled at the glowing pumpkin.

"No! It is you that have gone back on your word to help me. Now I am forced to follow another path," Jack replied.

Gus stood by the mailbox, looking down a dirt path that snaked through a forest of tall grass. He noticed that it looked like Steven had started to clear the front yard but stopped. The DR was parked where it must have run out of gas. *But where is Steven?* He decided to walk the dirt path to the back of the lot. *Maybe he is taking a break. His truck is still here.*

As he walked, it hit him; he was reliving his nightmare, the football game in the fog, scoring the touchdown, walking the tracks, and now the dirt path that led to… a backyard full of pumpkins climbing out of the ground. Some were using needles from their vines to carve out makeshift faces in their heads and opening their crown as a lid while a piece of hell's coal was placed in each newly carved skull. Now standing before him was an army of jack-o'-lanterns. Steven was lying on the ground inside the house of broken glass next to his mother.

"Mom!" His tongue was quicker than his mind.

Every flaming skull turned toward Gus. Gus's heart stopped momentarily and then began pounding within his chest.

Hundreds of orange pumpkins with poorly carved-out faces stepped toward him with their twisted vine legs. Their movements were abrupt and jerky, like a newborn colt just getting its legs underneath them for the first time. Flames shot out of the mouths of some as they struggled for control and collapsed back to the ground. Gus knew why his mother was there, but he did not know how to stop it from happening. *Now what do I do? We're dead meat!*

———

The Prince of Darkness glanced at Jack, stepping forward to examine the goods more thoroughly. He saw the thick leather binding of the large book in Jack's gnarled hands of vine and placed his finger under Margie's chin and gently tilted her head upward into the light so that he could see the face of the witch who had dared betray him.

"You are a master witch indeed. Remarkable really, considering the temporal nature of man. You have preserved yourself very well in this young disguise, but you still resemble your true self. Impressive." The devil wheeled toward Jack. "Yes, I accept this exchange. Now"—Satan pulled out his iconic fork as the devil prepared to finish his dealings with Jack once and for all—"I will seal our bargain with her blood!"

"No!"

Grandma Bertie entered the cavern through the corridor that originated in the wall of her barn. Molly raced to her side from behind the stacked crates where she had been hiding.

"She is not the one you desire. She is not the one whom you seek. Her blood is of no use to you. Only one who freely gives it will bring this matter to its proper end." Jack and the devil stared at her closely. They recognized the conviction in her voice and her features.

"Marguarette?" Jack was in shock. He had not seen her in over 150 years. The devil snarled, annoyed by the delayed victory.

Gus turned and quickly ran back to Steven's truck. He grabbed all that he could carry. He stuffed two machetes into his pants at the waist and picked up the commercial-grade Weed Eater. The engine roared to life after the fifth pull on the starter cord. With a determined scowl, Gus reentered the yard with conviction.

"Stay away from my mother, you flamin' freaks!"

Gus blazed a trail toward his mother and Steven, cutting down every walking gourd that dared come close. With a whip of his wrist, their legs vanished under the toppling gourds. He swung his spinning weapon, splitting several pumpkins before they could regenerate or emerge from the ground. He threatened the rest as he made his way toward Steven and his mother, making sure that they were all in front of him at a good distance.

One jack-o'-lantern came at Gus from his right flank; Gus raised his weapon and decapitated it. The head rolled to his feet. Its eyes were round, and its mouth was a simple slit across its face. It had no nose, Gus noticed before he leapt into the air, landing on top of it, crushing the skull. This agitated the others all the more.

Steven stood and helped Janice to her feet. Gus backed his way to them, keeping the jack-o'-lanterns at a distance with every swing of the Weed Eater.

"Hi, Mom." Gus smiled, looking at the both of them. "Follow me. I'm going to get us out of here." Just then, the Weed Eater began to sputter and died.

"Oh no!"

"You didn't fill it up?" Steven asked.

"I didn't have time! Quick, inside! Steven, grab those!" Gus said, pointing to the hand clippers and the shovel that were on the ground under the table in the center of the glass house.

Every gruesome carved-out face began to grin and move closer. The jack-o'-lanterns surrounded them inside the glass house and began smashing all of the panes of glass to get at them. Steven handed Janice the clippers for protection. One jack-o'-lantern stuck his flaming skull inside and screamed. "We're going to pull you up by the roots, boy! Then we will drain you and your friends of every drop!" Its eyes flickered with delight.

"I don't think so!" Gus pulled out his machetes from his waistband and whacked the screamer's head off. Steven slammed the rolling head with his shovel, shattering it in several pieces.

"Grandma Bertie is the Witch of Willow Branch?" Margie and Molly gasped. Bertie moved closer toward Margie. Jack and the devil stood dumbfounded, watching her in amazement. She gathered the children behind her, putting herself between them and the devil.

The threesome in the house of shattered glass flipped over the table that sat in the middle of the tiny space. Gus whirled his machetes like a ninja, cutting off arms and legs as they presented themselves through the broken panels of glass. Steven used the edge of his shovel to do the same on the opposite side of the table.

A rogue vine crept its way past them, weaving itself around the neck of Janice, who was still weak and had closed her eyes for a moment. She reacted in haste with all of her remaining strength and snipped the vine in two.

Vines from behind him grabbed Gus's wrists and jerked the blades away from him as the monsters continued their attack from all directions. Steven fought them off, pounding and slicing vines and hollow pumpkin heads with ugly, nasty faces, until one pierced his neck with a black needle and finally ripped Steven's weapon from his grasp.

Steven dropped down to shield Janice, who was huddled in the dead center of the room as the jack-o'-lanterns swarmed inside. Vines lashed out at them from all directions, coiling around them, binding their arms and legs together. One jack-o'-lantern looked Gus in the eyes, its lopsided mouth grinning as a long black needle shot up in front of Gus's face from the tip of its finger. There was no escaping their fate.

―――――――――

"If it is my blood you seek, then you may have it, but you will never have my children!" Bertie said.

The devil grinned; he could smell victory as he gripped his fork tighter. "We shall see about that. But as of now, you are mine!" Bertie winced as he thrust his fork.

"No!" three voices burst out in synchrony.

Satan's fork sunk deep and found blood. It streamed down the shaft of the pitchfork, inching toward Satan's hands. His smile of satisfaction melted away as he realized what had happened.

"*What have you done?*" The devil howled.

His fork had struck Jack, who had lunged in front of Grandma Bertie, shielding her from the blow. Jack was pierced through the back with the barbs of the fork poking out the front of his chest. Satan quickly freed his fork from its unintended target.

"Once more for the road, ol' boy. I stuck it to *you*... once more for the road," Jack managed to whisper as he collapsed into Bertie's arms, and the jack-o'-lantern transformed back into a man.

Gus felt light-headed, as if he were going to pass out, as the black needle sank into his flesh. The world was spinning before his eyes, Gus was feeling faint. Suddenly, every flaming, bloodsucking jack-o'-lantern shrieked as their vines began to wither; some of their heads dried up and shriveled, while others imploded and still others exploded.

When they opened their eyes, they were covered with sticky pieces of pumpkin; seeds and greenery were scattered everywhere. They looked at one another in disbelief and yelled for joy. Gus hugged his mother for the first time in a very long time.

He looked her in the eyes then turned toward Steven, who was sitting, leaning back upon his hands.

"What just happened?" Gus asked.

"That's an excellent question…for your grandmother," Steven said as he collapsed backward to the ground in exhaustion.

Jack's selfless and sacrificial act of love had finally broken his curse. He had always been a conniver, and he had planned this final scene of scenarios to ultimately work in his favor so that he would be free of the devil once and for all.

He had made his deal with the devil once he discovered the *Book of Spells*. He then encouraged Margie to learn the spell that could bring her mother back to life, hoping that she would be willing to use him as a safety test and therefore he could bypass the devilish deal that he had made earlier. What he did not expect was for another course of action to present itself—one that, until Margie had hidden her notes inside of a Bible and placed them in the hollow of a root in the chamber at the base of the Shelter Tree, he had never known existed before. And of course, he had never expected Grandma Bertie, the woman formerly known as Roberta Marguarette Smythe, Jack's wife and the Witch of Willow Branch, who now held him in her arms.

Tears streamed down her face as she searched his eyes for answers and hope for this man who had saved her from Satan's stinging wrath.

The devil howled in defiance as two huge glowing figures appeared in the cavern with them all; they were supernatural beings sent from the heavenly realms to escort Satan back to his temporary home.

"I'll get you! I'll get you all! You will pay for what you have done if it is the last thing I ever do!" He vanished into a great ball of light.

Jack's eyes met Bertie's for the first time in over 150 years. "I'm sorry," he breathed, gasping for air. "I'm so sorry. You deserved better...better than me. I couldn't let you pay for my debt again. I know it's too late, but I do love you, Marguarette. I love you. Please forgive me."

"It's not too late. It's never too late for reconciliation, Jack. I do forgive you," Bertie said as she laid Jack's head slowly on the floor. His eyes had closed for the final time. "I did love you, Jack." His body disintegrated into dust on the ground as another great sphere of light appeared in the room.

Bertie heard Jack's voice in her head. *Thank you, Marguarette. You showed me love and mercy in my lifetime. Thank Margie as well. It was her compassion and her foresight in placing that Bible where I would find it that allowed me to know the truth, and it has now set me free. "This is how we know the love of God: because he laid down his life for us, and we should lay down our lives for the brethren." I understand now, and I finally see. I no longer have to hide behind your love and mercy to save me from my debt anymore. I have accepted God's true love and mercy, and my debt is wiped away—forever. So please do not weep for me, Marguarette.*

Bertie saw his face one last time within the great ball of light, and then his voice and the sphere were gone. Bertie wiped the tears from her eyes in vain. She hugged Margie and Molly with every ounce of might she could muster.

It was finished.

The Curse of the Jack-O'-Lantern had been broken forevermore.

EPILOGUE

In the pit, Satan sat on his temporary throne, still seething from Jack's final act of trickery. He glanced down at the thick book still in his hands.

"I mustn't be too hard upon myself. After all, I am not empty-handed. The *Book of Spells* is back in my possession."

He opened the thick, leather cover. His eyes began to blaze with anger. He saw that page after page of white-ruled notebook paper with handwritten spells in pink and purple ink were stuffed inside a hollowed-out Bible.

"A copy? *What treachery is this?*" Satan roared, as the delicate binding and its pages turned to ash in a flash in the extreme heat, leaving the devil empty-handed.

"*No!*"